D1593972

BLIND SIDED

LINDSAY MCKENNA

Blue Turtle Publishing

Praise for Lindsay McKenna

"A treasure of a book ... highly recommended reading that everyone will enjoy and learn from."

—Chief Michael Jaco, US Navy SEAL, retired, on Breaking Point

"Readers will root for this complex heroine, scarred both inside and out, and hope she finds peace with her steadfast and loving hero. Rife with realistic conflict and spiced with danger, this is a worthy page-turner."

—BookPage.com on Taking Fire
March 2015 Top Pick in Romance

"... is fast-paced romantic suspense that renders a beautiful love story, start to finish. McKenna's writing is flawless, and her story line fully absorbing. More, please."

—Annalisa Pesek, Library Journal on Taking Fire

"Ms. McKenna masterfully blends the two different paces to convey a beautiful saga about love, trust, patience and having faith in each other."

—Fresh Fiction on Never Surrender

"Genuine and moving, this romantic story set in the complex world of military ops grabs at the heart."

—RT Book Reviews on Risk Taker

"McKenna does a beautiful job of illustrating difficult topics through the development of well-formed, sympathetic characters."

—Publisher's Weekly (starred review) on Wolf Haven
One of the Best Books of 2014, Publisher's Weekly

"McKenna delivers a story that is raw and heartfelt. The relationship between Kell and Leah is both passionate and tender. Kell is the hero every woman wants, and McKenna employs skill and s empathy to craft a physically and emotionally abused character in Leah. Using tension and steady pacing, McKenna is adept at expressing growing, tender love in the midst of high stakes danger."

—RT Book Reviews on Taking Fire

"Her military background lends authenticity to this outstanding tale, and readers will fall in love with the upstanding hero and his fierce determination to save the woman he loves.

—Publishers Weekly (starred review) on Never Surrender
One of the Best Books of 2014, Publisher's Weekly

"Readers will find this addition to the Shadow Warriors series full of intensity and action-packed romance. There is great chemistry between the characters and tremendous realism, making Breaking Point a great read."

—RT Book Reviews

"This sequel to Risk Taker is an action-packed, compelling story, and the sizzling chemistry between Ethan and Sarah makes this a good read."

—RT Book Reviews on Degree of Risk

"McKenna elicits tears, laughter, fist-pumping triumph, and most all, a desire for the next tale in this powerful series."

—Publishers Weekly (starred review) on Running Fire

"McKenna's military experience shines through in this moving tale . . . McKenna (High Country Rebel) skillfully takes readers on an emotional journey into modern warfare and two people's hearts."

—Publisher's Weekly on Down Range

Lindsay McKenna has proven that she knows what she's doing when it comes to these military action/romance books."

—Terry Lynn, Amazon on Zone of Fire.

"At no time do you want to put your book down and come back to it later! Last Chance is a well written, fast paced, short (remember that) story that will please any military romance reader!"

—LBDDiaries, Amazon on Last Chance.

Also available from
Lindsay McKenna

Blue Turtle Publishing

DELOS

Last Chance, prologue novella to Nowhere to Hide
Nowhere To Hide, Book 1
Tangled Pursuit, Book 2
Forged in Fire, Book 3

2016
Broken Dreams, Book 4
Cowboy Justice Bundle/Blind Sided, Bundle 2, novella
Secret Dream, 1B novella, epilogue to Nowhere to Hide
Unbound Pursuit, 2B novella, epilogue to Tangled Pursuit
Dog Tags for Christmas Bundle/Snowflake's Gift, Bundle 3, novella

2017
Never Enough, 3B, novella, epilogue to Forged in Fire
Dream of Me novella, epilogue to Broken Dreams
Hold On, Book 5

Harlequin/HQN/Harlequin
Romantic Suspense

SHADOW WARRIORS
Danger Close
Down Range
Risk Taker

Degree of Risk
Breaking Point
Never Surrender
Zone of Fire
Taking Fire
On Fire
Running Fire

THE WYOMING SERIES

Shadows From The Past
Deadly Identity
Deadly Silence
The Last Cowboy
The Wrangler
The Defender
The Loner
High Country Rebel
Wolf Haven
Night Hawk
Out Rider

WIND RIVER VALLEY SERIES, Kensington

2016
Wind River Wrangler

2017
Wind River Rancher
Wind River Cowboy

Dear Reader,

Being an Indie is fun! I get to create novellas like *Blind Sided* for Cowboy Justice, a 12-pack bundle of novellas from twelve authors. The set includes TWELVE COWBOY LAWMEN who are so hot it should be criminal. The authors include me and eleven of my fabulous friends: Becky McGraw, Elle James, Donna Michaels, Lexi Post, Cynthia D'Alba, Susan Stoker, Delilah Devlin, Sable Hunter, Sabrina York, Randi Alexander, and Beth Williamson! I'm delighted to be with these eleven cowgirls who are some of the BEST storytellers in the business!

My addition is a Delos Series novella I created just for this 12-pack! *Blind Sided* is about a Texas deputy sheriff, Cade Patterson, who has loved Kara Knight from afar. Kara runs the Delos Home School in Clayton, Texas. Born into a wealthy family, she has been controlled by her father until she was eighteen. Now, at twenty-six, when Cade walks back into her life, everything changes. Her father called him trash from the wrong side of the tracks when they were teenagers but her heart knows different. The past collides with the present. Can their unrequited love blossom? Or will shadowy family secrets destroy any hope of a future that Kara desperately wants with this heroic Texas deputy?

Dedication

To Rae Nobel, a wonderful, long-time reader of mine. She started reading my very first books in the early 1980's. Sadly, she passed in December 2015, but I wanted to dedicate this story to her because I know she's up there, reading them!

Bless you, Rae. You are the best!

CHAPTER 1

Kara Knight felt the cinderblock Delos Home School vibrate beneath the rumble of a late Friday afternoon South Texas thunderstorm and grinned. She loved thunderstorms! She hurried from one classroom to another, making sure the windows were closed and locked. The winds gusted, pounding against the windows as Kara quickly shut each one. The July thunderstorm had met nothing but flat land with some rolling bumps, picking up energy and power from the nearby Gulf.

Loving the sound of the thunder, but hating the damage these storms could cause, Kara raced through the five classrooms and out into the kitchen and maintenance areas. There, she grabbed a huge dust mop. Her charity school was only one-story high. Since she had built it near economically deprived Clayton, it had flourished.

Earlier, the children's parents had arrived at

the school's day care center before the storm hit. Molly, the latest hire and a teacher, had felt a sudden migraine coming on, rendering her dizzy and unable to do much of anything. Blaine, her fellow teacher, had driven Molly back to Clayton, the nearby town where they all lived. That left Kara to clean up the day care area and prep it for Saturday, when Blaine was scheduled to come in to assist with the children at the day care.

Her career as a teacher had been a major disappointment to her father, Jud Knight. His prejudice against anyone with less money than he had always hung over her head. She hated her father's arrogance toward those who were poor and struggling. Thank goodness her mother, Pamela, was the opposite! She had supported her daughter's dream of helping these underprivileged children get three square meals a day plus an education. Kara wasn't sure what she'd have done if her Mom's support hadn't been there.

Kara learned about her mother's background over time. She revealed that she'd come from a hardscrabble family and had hauled herself up through the ranks to become the owner of Clayton's favorite, super-successful bakery. Kara's father had met her, admired her spunk and her ability to create luscious baked goods and a thriving business, and wooed her until she gave in and married him.

Kara was just like her mom—feisty, independent, and wanting to make a difference in her community. Thank goodness Pamela had given the green light to Kara's desire to be a teacher. She also supported her wish to work with Delos, the world's largest charity organization, to bring a school and a day care center to this impoverished area of Texas. At a career fair at Texas A&M University in College Station, Kara had met the Delos people and instantly decided to work with them. Their eighteen hundred worldwide charities were not only in foreign countries, but also in the U.S.

Hunger and a lack of education were here also, and it was something Kara wanted to change in her own state. They offered her a job, gave her the help and funds to construct the Home School Foundation building in Clayton, plus add an all-important day care center. For Kara it was a match made in heaven. She felt as if she had the best job in the world because it was personally fulfilling to her on every level.

All her life, Kara had tried to ignore her controlling father's harsh ways and words. Jud Knight was nasty, selfish, arrogant, and worth forty million dollars. His fellow Kenedy County citizens were well aware of his worth and the power of his influence. For that reason, during her four years of high school in Clayton, Kara had felt cursed by her father's overbearing personality. When he decided she should be homecoming queen during her junior year— voila! She was homecoming queen.

When he wanted her to be a cheerleader, despite her lack of interest in being one—again, she found herself selected, even though she hadn't even tried out like the other girls. She argued heatedly with her father, telling him she didn't want it, that it wasn't fair to the other girls who wanted to be a one. His abrupt answer was, "You're better than they are. They're all trailer trash." Later, in her room, she'd cried in frustration, wanting anonymity, not popularity, because she was a shy introvert by nature. Her father didn't care.

Outdoors, she heard the sudden pounding of small hailstones on the roof as she continued to clean up the huge day care facility. The last thing she'd do after sweeping and mopping, would be to arrange the desks for tomorrow morning. Everything had to be clean and ready to go for the nine a.m. arrival of the children on Saturday morning. She saw a flash of lightning so close that she winced, closing her eyes.

Suddenly, a man's hand wrapped around Kara's mouth, yanking her backwards off her feet. Her arms flailed and pain raced across her jaw where he gripped her. Kara tried to scream, but the man wrapped his other thick, hairy arm around her waist, pinning her against him.

"Shut up, bitch!" he snarled into her ear. His breath smelled of onions, making Kara want to gag. She struggled, kicking out, her arms trapped beneath the man's powerfully muscled arm. He began jerking her side to side, and she felt as if he were trying to rip her head off her shoulders. Her mind reeled as he continued to drag her backwards, keeping her off balance. She heard him curse at her in Spanish.

"I'll kill you, bitch. Now, stand still!" He pinched her nose shut with his thumb and forefinger, his hand still across her mouth, effectively shutting off her ability to breathe.

Gurgling in terror, her throat aching with a silent scream, her vision began to dim, and she fought harder, knowing she was going to die. *Oh, God! No! No!*

Black dots began to dance before her eyes as she began to pass out. Desperately, Kara lifted the heel of her boot, slamming it with all her might into the man's foot. He howled with pain, letting her go.

Free! She was free! Barely conscious, Kara fell to her knees, then scrambled to get away on all fours. She heard him cursing. Outdoors, another thunderclap shook the air.

Escape! I have to escape!

Air exploded from her mouth as she wobbled to her feet, weaving, her balance off, as she turned toward her attacker. He was a stranger. His brown eyes were dark with fury, his black hair was short and close-cropped, and he was barely taller than she. He appeared to be in his late twenties. He had black tattoos around his thick, bull-like neck and down both his powerful arms. A gold ring hung from his left earlobe. He wore a white muscle shirt, showing off the bulky muscling, scaring her even more. There was no doubt this man lifted very heavy weights at a gym. His jeans were well worn and his combat boots, scuffed. He looked like a soldier to her. She saw a knife in a sheath against his left calf and the pistol he wore in a drop holster around his right thigh. The only thing missing was a set of dog tags around his neck. Instead, he wore a thick gold chain.

Shrieking, Kara tried to dodge his hand as his fist closed, his arm drawn back to strike her. Her mind wasn't working right, deprived of oxygen, sodden with adrenaline. All she knew was that he was trying to kill her.

Why? Why is this horrible man trying to hurt me?

The moment his fist connected with the left side of her face, Kara heard a snapping sound, as if a huge branch of a tree had been broken inside her head, and everything went black. The last thing she remembered was sailing through the air, her arms wind-milling. And then, nothing.

SHERIFF'S DEPUTY CADE Patterson was waiting out the hellacious late afternoon thunderstorm. His cruiser was parked near the outskirts of Clayton as he watched the threatening sky become more and more ominous looking. There were tornado warnings out for the county, so he watched for any forming funnel cloud. Now it was dark, roiling, and ugly, lightning lacing, and turbulent clouds scudding swiftly across the dark sky.

The residents of Clayton, all thirty-five hundred of them, had sought shelter. Cade continued to keep an eye out for activity through his windshield, the wipers whipping back and forth in rhythmic time like a metronome. It was four p.m.—only an hour to go on his eight-hour shift as he sat behind the wheel and watched his white cruiser get its dusty surface blown away by the building winds.

There were two towns located at the east and west ends of Kenedy County. Although he lived in Sarita, the eastern town, his shift change would occur in Clayton, the western town. Then he'd drive twenty miles east down the two-lane highway to his home in Sarita. Having the weekend off was rare, and Cade had plans to rent a boat out at Padre Island and spend the weekend trolling for fish and then freezing his catch.

He dropped his black police Stetson onto the passenger side seat, wanting to get comfortable in his khaki long-sleeved shirt and dark blue trousers as he sat waiting out the storm. Cade put on his black baseball cap, which identified him as a deputy, preferring it to the Stetson if he had to go outside in this kind of weather.

As a kid, he'd liked thunderstorms, enjoying

the display of nature's wild fury, but not any more. He looked out at the gathering storm. In some ways, the explosiveness of the lightning combined with the pounding thunder reminded him of his black ops combat deployments in Afghanistan.

His mind flowed back to that time. He'd been in the Marine Corps from ages eighteen to twenty-four and he still considered himself a Marine, even if he was out of the service. *Once a Marine, always a Marine.* Wiping his shadowed cheeks with his hand, he remembered every mission behind enemy lines. As a covert spotter, he'd guide F-16 Air Force combat jets or A-10 Warthogs to Taliban targets, where they would drop their ordinances on the enemy. He liked being in black ops and he had been damned good at it. It never bothered Cade's conscience that the Taliban died in those air strikes. They were the enemy—one more group of evildoers that would no longer be alive to injure, kidnap, or kill peaceful Afghan villagers.

Drawing in a deep breath, his thoughts moved farther back in time, though he resisted it. Cade did *not* want to go back to his childhood here in Clayton. His straight black brows drew downward. In the first eighteen years of his life here in this town near the Mexican border, there had always been one person who'd brightened his life.

Just the memory of Kara Knight's large blue

eyes fringed with long, sable lashes made Cade's heart fill with yearning. His mouth thinned as he felt those old emotions bubble up to the surface. Why the hell couldn't he just forget her? She'd been forbidden fruit for someone like him—a young man poor as a church mouse.

His dad, Walt Patterson, had established a plumbing business here in Clayton shortly after Cade was born. Twelve years later, Walt died suddenly of a heart attack. Cade and his mother, Tracy, lost everything: the man they both loved and depended on, the business that had been their only source of income, and finally, their home.

Tracy had been a stay-at-home mom because Walt had made enough money to allow it. But twelve-year-old Cade had no idea at the time how the world of finances worked; now, life would give him an accelerated course in the subject.

The day his father died, Cade's life changed forever. His anger still sparked deep within him when he remembered Jud Knight, the richest man in the county, dropping by during visiting hours at the funeral home. He had a sneer on his thick, fleshy lips, his green eyes close set together, his narrow face arrogant looking. Cade had never liked Jud. His god was money, not people. Everything was measured by how much money you made and that was it.

Jud Knight had entered the visitor's room and approached his mother, sitting on a couch alone with Cade's thin arm around her shoulder.

"Damn, I'm sorry for your loss, Mrs. Patterson," he rasped. "Clayton doesn't have a plumber any more and we're all in the shitter, if you get my drift." Then, he spun around and left.

Cade had sat there, staring after the short, lean Texan who had once been a state champion bronco rider. At eighteen, Jud's father, Gordon Knight, had made his son foreman of the Circle K Ranch. From then on, he became an egotistical rich man who disdained the "trash" of Clayton. He made no apologies for his brutal manner and he spat out "the truth" as he saw it.

Cade's mother began to cry as Jud stalked off, the white embroidered hanky in her hand pressed to her eyes. And then, less than fifteen minutes later, Pamela Knight, Jud's wife, entered wearing an elegant black dress with tasteful gold jewelry. Cade's heart had leaped because her daughter, Kara, was at her side, looking wan and sad. Her soulful blue gaze met his and Cade felt tears jamming into his eyes. Fighting them back, he clung to Kara's gaze, seeing the shyness in her delicate face.

Her sable hair was in a set of pigtails, small gold ribbons tied down at the end of each one. She too, wore a black dress that hung just below her knees. Kara looked beautiful to Cade. He felt some of the heaviness in his heart lift as her lower lip trembled and she gave him a small, shy smile of hello.

They never spoke to one another at school—they didn't dare. Cade knew she was off limits to all but the rich boys. But at that moment he could swear that she was silently reaching out to comfort him. That moment was branded forever into his aching heart.

Pamela Knight had come over and gently patted his mother's shaking shoulder, whispering heartfelt words of comfort to her. Kara had stood nearby, her gaze fastened on the floor, her small hands nervously gripping each other. Cade even remembered the black shoes she'd worn, and the black tights on her spindly legs. Her arms were ghostly against the darkness of the dress she wore and she looked scared. How Cade wanted to comfort her! But his mother needed him, so he stayed put.

He was mesmerized as Kara lifted her tiny, stubborn looking chin and boldly stared straight at him for a moment. They'd gone to grade school together, and now they were both in the seventh grade, but because she was the daughter of Jud Knight, he knew to leave her alone.

Jud had made it clear that the townspeople of Clayton were little more than white and brown trash. This part of Texas was filled with illegal immigrants in the area searching for a better life in America. Half the town was Latino and most of them were undocumented. The other half of the town was struggling white Texans. Knight had an "us against them," attitude toward the

Latinos, and utter disdain for the whites.

Cade had been raised not to see color. To him, every human being "bled red" and everyone had feelings and a heart that could be wounded. His father had taught him early on that everyone deserved respect, regardless of their economic status. Walt had been a Marine, serving his country before settling down to earn his livelihood as a plumber, and Cade was proud of his dad, who was half Comanche and half white. His father had the same skin color as their Latino neighbors on the poor side of their small town. Cade grew up with the same coloring as his father's, never thinking anything about it until Jud Knight had embarrassed the hell out of him in the feed store when he was nine-years-old.

"Hey, Patterson," Knight called across the busy store to his father, "what'd you do, take in one of those trashy illegals? Adopt the kid, maybe?"

His father quietly came over and told Knight to take his dirty mouth and get the hell out of the store or he'd do it for him. Cade remembered his head swiveling from one man's expression to the other and briefly thought he detected fear suddenly leap into Knight's narrowed eyes. He could feel his father's rage barely in control, revealed only by his low, growling voice. He knew his father could clean Knight's clock without a problem. His father was a Marine and Marines always protected those they loved.

Knight left abruptly, stomping out of Garcia's feed store, leaving a stilted vacuum in his absence. Cade felt his father's hand on his shoulder, warm and supportive. "Come on son, let's go get that feed your mother needs for our cow, Bess."

Nodding jerkily, Cade was glad his father turned, bringing him alongside him, arm around his tiny shoulders, protecting him from the eyes of so many other men in the store, watching as Jud had embarrassed him. He remembered looking down at his skin, that golden hue he'd always considered a beautiful color, especially when sunlight glanced off it. No, he wasn't white like Jud Knight. What confused Cade was that the man knew that he was Walt Patterson's son. It was then that he decided Knight was just a mean, evil person. And he'd never changed his mind about him since then. Cade already knew that the rancher called them trash because his father made a living as a plumber.

Wrenching his thoughts back to the present, Cade stared up at the ceiling of his cruiser, listening to the pounding rain that had enveloped Clayton, cleansing it. He surrendered, the memories insisting on flooding through him.

One of his fondest memories happened at his father's funeral. Half the town came through that evening, paying their final, heartfelt respects to Walt Patterson. Military vets who were now civilians stopped at his open coffin and snapped to attention, saluting him. Others reached out to touch his cold, clasped hands. Some stood there, as if remembering something special about his father, tears in their eyes.

Cade's heart pounded with so much grief, so much loss. He would never see his father's wide grin again or hear that deep laughter that always made him smile in return. More than anything, his father loved him and his mother with a fierceness that defied words. Cade felt as if his world had been torn in two, never to be the same again.

It was when Kara Knight had shyly moved forward, her hand extended uncertainly toward him, lightly grazing his cheek, holding his startled gaze as he looked up. There were tears in her luminous blue eyes. In that moment, Cade felt as if they had made a magical connection with one another. He physically *felt* her care for him, her sadness for the loss of his beloved father, and that she wanted to help him in whatever way she could.

Without a word, she stepped forward as Pamela Knight chatted with his mother and wrapped her thin arms around his shoulder, pulling him forward so his head rested against her chin. Kara squeezed him as tightly as she possibly could, whispering, "I'm so sorry, Cade…so sorry. Your father was a great man, not like mine." And then, she pressed her lips to his forehead in an innocent kiss.

Dragging in a ragged breath, Cade closed his eyes as the rain poured down even harder, the cruiser cloaked in a gray fog so he could see nothing around him. Kara's warmth, her kindness at that moment, remained with him forever. It was the first and only time he'd been touched by her. His skin where she'd pressed that soft kiss still tingled as he remembered how it felt, and the scent of her sweet honeysuckle fragrance.

Even now, well over a decade later, Cade could still feel the warmth of her arms around him, hauling him tightly against her, feeling as if she were trying to transfer her love to him to protect him from the savage grief tearing through him. It was as if Kara knew how he felt inside, and he could feel her giving herself to him. That stunned him. As nasty and belligerent as her father Jud was, Kara was the complete opposite. He remembered sliding his free arm around her slender waist, holding on to her like a life preserver. She gave him so much in that one moment that to this day, it made his heart yearn for Kara.

When he'd returned to Clayton after leaving the Marine Corps, his mother had mentioned Kara to him. How could she know he held a dream of having her in his life? He was old enough at that time to know that women had their ways. And his mother, who worked part time at the local McDonald's since his father had died, would always give him that mysterious smile.

Even in the Marine Corps, she'd email him to share the latest town gossip, and always mentioned Kara to him, as if keeping her at the front and center of his attention, not allowing him to forget her. His mother must have known that the one time little Kara had hugged him, trying to make him feel better even though his father was dead, something special had passed between them.

And Cade had been running from it ever since.

Knowing he needed to find a job after leaving the Corps, Cade had gone to the local community college to get a two-year law enforcement degree. His father had taught him to save his money starting from a young age. What he didn't send to his mother of his monthly paycheck while in the Corps, he put into a bank account. By the time his enlistment was up, he had money to buy a house. He wanted to work for the Kenedy County Sheriff's Department. With his background in black ops, Cade knew it was a good fit and so did Sheriff Parker. The gruff, sixty-five-year-old with a white handlebar mustache, had offered him a job immediately after his graduation. Another thing in his favor was that he was bilingual. He could speak Spanish as well as English. From time to time, his mother asked him if he'd seen Kara around. He said no, he hadn't. His life now revolved around getting that degree, studying, and more studying. He had no time for a personal life yet.

Besides, he told his mother, Kara was off limits to him. She just gave him that secretive smile and noted that Kara was still single, even though her daddy had tried to marry her off to several rich men over the years.

Cade didn't take the bait. He couldn't. There was no way he was going to fight Jud Knight for his daughter.

After graduation, he bought a small home in Sarita, the headquarters for the sheriff's department. He knew Kara worked at the Delos Home School, but fought the desire to see her. Getting a home twenty miles east of Clayton kept the distance he wanted. Sometimes, he had shifts where he worked out of his hometown of Clayton, like tonight. But he'd still get his gear, climb out of his uniform in the locker room, and get into civilian clothes before driving home.

That was twenty miles away from Kara Knight, because she now lived in the Latino quarter of this town. His heart pined for her, the longing so intense on some nights that it woke him up. Just once-as an adult now, not as a scared, grieving little boy, he wanted to go see her. But he was afraid of being rejected by her if he reappeared into her life.

There were times in high school when they would pass one another in the busy, noisy hall between classes. Kara was always popular at school, a cheerleader, surrounded by other girls who had affluent parents like her own. She always seemed ill at ease around the other girls who were like princesses vying for the queen's attention.

Kara was actually shy, like him. Sometimes, he would be pressed against the lockers, books in hand, watching her entourage pass him by. She was always the center of attention. But it had been that way because her father was rich and powerful. Often Cade wanted to ask Kara how she felt about that, because all the attention seemed to drain her, just as it did to him.

There were rare moments when Cade would be outside the multi-story red brick school, jogging across the grass, heading to or from school, and he'd catch sight of her. She never wore clothes that were sexy looking, like so many other high school girls did. Prim and proper, she stood out because her clothing was modest. He remembered his mother saying that Jud Knight had uniforms made for her to wear to hide her body so boys wouldn't be tempted to chase her. But Cade always looked at Kara anyway. He didn't care what kind of clothing she wore.

And sometimes he got lucky and she'd lift that delicate, stubborn chin of hers, those wide blue eyes meeting and holding his longing stare. It was at those times when electricity seemed to fly back and forth between them. He was too young, too immature to understand that giddy sensation that swallowed him whole after she tore her gaze from him. But his heart would always race with wild, joyous abandon.

Later, after he'd had several relationships with women after he'd joined the Marines, Cade had come to realize what those feelings were really all about. He'd been too young to decipher his happiness when Kara's gaze would accidentally meet his. And even now, Cade was afraid to name what he felt. He was old enough, at twenty-seven, to know what it was. But it could never be. He would never be financially wealthy. Jud Knight would always be disdainful of him. Yes, being a sheriff's deputy held respect in the community, but not with Knight. He tarred and feathered law enforcement right along with everyone else in the county.

Opening his eyes, Cade stared unseeing as the cruiser's windshield wipers swung back and forth, giving him glimpses of the gully-washing storm as it dumped all its water on Clayton. His mind kept circling around to one question: why was Kara still single? He knew her father wanted her married off so she'd become a broodmare and give him grandsons. That was Jud's vision for his only daughter—the bearer of male progeny to run his damn ranch. Snorting softly with disdain, he moved around in his seat. Had her father run off all the suitors who had been interested in her? Had she spurned them? There were at least five times when that had happened, according to his matchmaking mother.

Was it her father who had broken up the relationships? Cade had thought so, and his mother said the same thing when he'd come home after leaving the Corps. As badly as he felt pushed by invisible hands to go see Kara, to find out what really was between them, if anything, Cade had resisted. He knew Jud Knight got into every man's face who showed any kind of interest in her. Those who tried got hurt and got the message. He had no desire to take on Knight.

But he did feel sorry for Kara. The men who were driven off by her father had been judged to not be good enough for her, his mother had told him. Cade couldn't understand why Kara tolerated her father's heavy-handedness, but he reminded himself that she'd grown up beneath his controlling, dark shadow and knew nothing else. Had this drive only been a youthful fantasy? Yet, he'd had enough relationships in the military to know that what lay deep in his heart wasn't fleeting.

Ever since Kara had held him with her child's love and strength at that funeral parlor, Cade had been totally smitten by her.

His radio blared to life and he cocked his head toward it.

"Code 217 in progress at Delos Home School, Clayton," the Sarita dispatcher announced over the radio. "Will the closest cruiser respond? Over."

Frowning, Cade pressed the receiver on the radio he carried on his left shoulder. A code 217 was an assault with intent to murder. "Copy that, car twenty-two. I'm about a mile from there. I'll take the call. Out."

It was four-thirty p.m. The pall of rain was letting up. He flipped the lights on and put the vehicle into gear and swiftly drove the cruiser onto the highway. He knew exactly where that school was located. So who had turned in the burglary call? Who was at the school this late on a Friday afternoon?

CHAPTER 2

RAW PAIN SHOT up through Kara's face as she sat down on a chair in the day care center, gripping her cellphone in her hand. Her attacker had left. Or had he? Warily, she looked around, but her gaze was fastened on the opened door and entrance to the day care area. Stunned and hurting after regaining consciousness, she'd crawled to the chair and pulled her phone from her pocket to call 9-1-1. Dizzy, her ears ringing, she tried without success to stop the blood from pouring out of her left nostril. It felt as if half her face had been ripped off. The heat, swelling, and pain making her whimper. She was hunched over, praying that someone, anyone, would get here fast to help her.

The dispatcher on the 9-1-1 line said a Kenedy County sheriff's cruiser was on its way. How far away was it though? Her hair hung like curtains on either side of her face as her bloody, slippery fingers carefully pressed against her nose. The pain was excruciating, so she stopped trying to examine the extent of her injury.

Shattered by the attack, Kara kept worrying that her assailant would come back. But everything was quiet in the day care center and out in the hall beyond it. The rain was slacking off, the thunder moving farther west, the storm passing quickly through the area. She heard the front door open and then close. Who was it? Her heart pounded hard in her chest. Was it the man coming back to finish her off? To kill her?

Stifling a cry, she straightened, tense in the chair, unable to walk much because her knees were feeling so weak. Her breath hitched as she saw a sheriff's deputy appear in the entrance, his revolver drawn. A gasp tore from Kara—she couldn't believe what she was seeing. The man wearing the black Stetson, dressed in a deputy's uniform, was none other than Cade Patterson! She'd heard through the county grapevine that he'd come home three years earlier, but she had never run into him or seen him. His shoulders were so broad that she longed to simply lay her head on them and collapse into his arms. His light brown eyes were large, wide set, and assessing her, holding her distraught gaze.

"Kara!" He looked as shocked as she did. "What happened? Is there anyone else here?" he asked urgently, his head swiveling to take in the room.

"A man attacked me from behind…I-I don't know why…" Her voice sounded young, like a scared child, not her normal alto tone. She saw that his eyes were filled with concern.

"Okay, stay where you are for a moment. I have to clear every room to make sure no one is still in here. I'll be right back."

She nodded. "I'm not going anywhere. I can't walk. I'm dizzy."

"I'll be right back," he promised.

Huge tears of relief squeezed out of her eyes. Kara wrapped her arms around herself, the blood dripping continuously down onto her white blouse, forever staining it. Cade was like a silent shadow, disappearing from her view as he moved down the hall, pistol drawn. Was her attacker still in here hiding? Waiting to jump her again? She felt so cold. So alone. And yet, Cade was here! He was the last person she'd ever expected to see and she was infinitely grateful it was him.

Kara had been hoping to see him on the street, maybe catch sight of him at the local diner or run into him at the grocery store. But she never had, until now. Gulping, hating the metallic taste of blood in her mouth, she swallowed, her stomach roiling.

"Kara?"

Cade's voice was so close to her, she snapped her head up, gasping, not hearing him return to her side. He stood before her, sliding his revolver into the holster.

Her hand flew to her throat as she stared up at him. How tall he was! She remembered the boy of eighteen. That was the last time she'd seen him. Even though Cade had played football, the coach was always after him to put on more muscle, but he never had. Her gaze traveled up, from his narrow hips encased in dark blue gabardine trousers to the light khaki-colored shirt that stretched across his broad chest. And those proud, straight shoulders of his that looked as if they could carry the weight of the world on them. She knew from Cade's hard, younger life, that he'd carried his mother who had been so broken by her husband's unexpected death.

Words stuck in her tight throat as he crouched down close to her, placing his hand tentatively upon her upper right arm, his gaze melting into hers.

"Broken nose?" he asked gently.

"I-I think so…he hit me. That's the last thing I remember."

"I'll call an ambulance," he said, his hand reluctantly leaving her arm so he could make the call from his shoulder radio.

She looked beyond him, panicked, as he ended the call. "Is he still here, Cade?"

Shaking his head, he said, "No, no one's here. We're alone. Are you hurt anywhere else, Kara?"

Just the low warmth, the concern in his eyes, brought more tears. She choked and sobbed, "I-I don't think so...I didn't expect this...I don't know who he was. He attacked me from behind. I got a look at him after I smashed his foot with my heel, just for a second before I tried to run from him." Cade's hand was stabilizing as he lightly moved it up and down her upper arm, as if to comfort her.

"We can cover all that later."

"God, I wish my nose would quit bleeding." She held up her bloodied fingers.

"Hold on," Cade murmured, rising. He pulled out a white linen handkerchief from his back pocket, slipping it into her hand. "Press two fingers gently against the root of your nose and pinch the area as much as you can without causing yourself more pain. It should slow and stop the bleeding," he said, crouching next to her once more.

Needing his comforting touch, she closed her eyes and held the handkerchief against her nose with one hand and pinched the root of her nose with the other. "I-I'm not hurt anywhere else. Bruised knees maybe, that's all."

Kara began to shake uncontrollably, barely holding herself together. Some of the bleeding was slowing down and that was good. Absorbing Cade's masculine nearness, she felt like a thief stealing his light, his energy. Listening to the low timbre of his voice as he spoke to the dispatcher requesting a forensics team and back up, she once more felt that powerful swell of protection embracing her. And yet, Cade was not even touching her! Missing his hand on her arm, she needed to connect with him once again. It was a wild, unbidden thought and she couldn't stop any of her rampant, twisting feelings from barreling through her right now.

Getting off his radio, Cade placed his hand on her shoulder and asked, "What can I get you? Anything? The ambulance will be here in about five minutes. It's coming from the Clayton Volunteer Fire Department."

"Just—you…I don't need anyone else. Please don't leave me, Cade." She was prattling on, her voice high, off pitch, sounding nearly hysterical. She felt his fingers press gently into her shoulder, some unnamed emotion burned in his eyes for a moment, stunning her. She was no longer a moon-eyed child in love with Cade Patterson from afar. That look he'd given her just now was filled with more than concern. It was something much, much more and shock of another kind moved through her.

"I won't leave you," he promised. "Just try to relax. You've been traumatized, Kara. Everything's going to be all right."

His voice was like smooth, warm sunlight calming the choppy waters of her frantic, raw emotions. "I-I'm so scared…this has never happened before. I don't understand it, Cade. I don't…"

"After a doctor examines you, Kara, I'll need

to take your statement. I'm not going to try to do it right now. You're too upset."

"I-I'll see you again, then?"

He smiled a little. "I'm like a bad cold. You won't get rid of me that easily." He saw her muster a faint, wobbly smile. She was physically trembling. "But let's get you to the ER first, okay? After the doc patches you up, we can talk about what happened here."

"I must look awful," she whispered.

"You're beautiful. Don't ever forget that. Blood can be wiped away. The doc will fix up your broken nose and you'll be just like new in no time."

She *was* beautiful to Cade. His words flowed powerfully through her, warming her pounding heart, soothing away some of her fear and anxiety. "I never saw myself like that…"

"Your beauty has always come from your heart and your kindness to others," Cade murmured, sliding his hand gently across her hunched shoulder.

Unhappily, she groaned, "I'm a mess, Cade. Look at my blouse. It's ruined!" She gestured at the bloody material.

"Cold water will wash it out. At least, that's what my mom always told me," and he gave her a crooked, bashful grin.

She felt so much warmth coming from Cade, all of it unspoken, so deep and quiet, hidden within him until this moment. It was as if he had placed an invisible, warm blanket around her shoulders, a gesture of deep caring. "Your mother is a wonderful person, Cade. I often see her at the grocery store and other places around Clayton," she said.

"When I was in the Marine Corps, my mother sort of kept me up on what was happening with you here in Clayton, Kara," he replied. Amusement filled his tone. "I learned the cold water trick in the Marine Corps, as well. Got into a bar fight once," he touched his own nose, "and broke it. The gunny sergeant had to talk to the local police department and plead to let us out of jail. Said he'd deal with us back at the naval station. He was the one that told me to clean up blood with cold water. Most gunnies are mother hens to the Marines they command."

"You broke your nose, too?" She stared at his face for a moment, seeing a slight bump on it.

"Yeah, not my finest moment in the Corps," he admitted wryly. "Is there someone I can contact for you to let them know about this attack, Kara?"

"No! I don't want you to call my father and tell him what happened to me." The words came out in a rush, filled with panic.

"Do you have someone else you'd rather me call? A man in your life? Your mother?"

Kara closed her eyes, dizziness sweeping through her. She hunkered down, pressing her back solidly against the chair, afraid she was going to pitch to the right for a second. Cade's hand became firmer, as if he sensed what she was experiencing. It was that mental telepathy, that magical connection between them that had always existed, vibrating between them. It was here again, right now.

And never had Kara been happier to feel it. She opened her eyes after a moment, looking into his narrowed gaze. He was worried for her. "I live alone. There's no one in my life." She gestured slightly to the day care area. "This is my passion. I love what I do here, helping the kids learn English."

"I'll have to notify your mom, then," he said, regret in his tone. "She'll want to know for sure."

"Okay," Kara agreed reluctantly. "Just ask her to come see me at the hospital, please. I-I can't handle my father's king-size drama anymore."

"Okay," he said, pulling his cellphone out of his pocket. "Give me her number and I'll give her a call after the ambulance arrives. It shouldn't take her long to get over to the hospital to see you."

"Good," she whispered, suddenly feeling so weak she could literally melt into a puddle. "I'm exhausted."

"It's the adrenaline leaving your system. We call it 'crashing.' It's a normal reaction to what you've experienced. Just sit and rest."

His reassurance helped steady her. Did Cade

know how calming he was for her? She had been hysterical before he arrived, sobbing and unable to stop crying. Again, she hung onto the soothing, deep timbre of his voice. It took away her fear and replaced it with a sense of safety she'd never known before now.

Cade had turned into a big man with a set of broad shoulders, not heavily muscled, but definitely in top shape. There was no fat on his body. Just the way he held himself in this crisis told her of his quiet strength. Tufts of black hair peeked above the white neckline of the T-shirt he wore beneath his shirt. Yes, Cade had grown into a man—a ruggedly handsome one, and it made her heart beat a little harder.

It was all so crazy! Kara was literally shaking from the adrenaline crash and he was holding her steady in the chair, his hand never leaving her arm. Emotions were whipsawing around, colliding with one another until she felt even wearier than before.

All she knew at this moment was that Cade would protect her. Every once in awhile, she would glance furtively toward the opened door, afraid that she'd see her assailant standing there. Cade, too, would routinely sweep his gaze around the room, to the entrance, the windows, as if expecting him to show up again, as well.

That frightened her, but she tried to stop the spiral downward into abject terror. She'd never been hit in her life and this had shattered her in many unexpected ways. Logically, she knew there was a police cruiser outside and that the man would probably see it and not come back to hurt her some more, but her emotions were running her right now.

The wail of the ambulance short-circuited the rest of her thoughts. Cade stood up, his hand tightening on her shoulder as if to keep her steady so she wouldn't fall out of the chair. Two EMTs from the Clayton Fire Department entered the facility with their medical bags in hand. They knew Cade and greeted him warmly.

Kara's world shifted when Cade stepped aside to allow the EMTs to examine and take care of her. She saw him walk to the entrance, keeping guard and remaining alert. She was relieved that he wasn't leaving and she gave her attention to the EMTs who crouched down in front of her. Her last, fleeting thought was that she wished she'd had more one-on-one time with Cade. How badly she wanted to talk to him alone.

Kara had dozens of questions for him. They'd been separated when she was eighteen and she was twenty-six now. That was a long time to be away from someone you'd cared for once. Really, Kara had never thought she'd see Cade again. Something old and hidden deep within her burst open now, sending rays of hope she'd thought had died when Cade had left.

Perhaps she might be able to connect with Cade now. After all, she didn't see a wedding ring on his finger. He was so good looking, confident, and gentle, Kara couldn't imagine him without a woman in his life. For a moment, her hopes were dampened. She recalled when she was young dreaming of Cade being the only boy she ever wanted in her life. But her wish hadn't come true. Then.

CADE HAD TO get a grip on himself. He felt as if a bomb had detonated inside him. He kept hearing Kara's soft, broken words. *Just—you…I don't need anyone else. Please don't leave me, Cade.*

He knew very well that people, when traumatized, tended to be honest about their feelings. In fact, people who hid behind masks often had them ripped off in a moment of shock. Kara's honesty cut deeply into his heart, reminding him how much he'd dreamed of her at his side for a lifetime when he was a teen.

Kara didn't wear a mask, nor was she manipulative, like her old man. Thankfully she'd never turned into a female version of crafty, greedy Jud Knight. Instead, she'd taken after her very kind, warm-hearted mother, Pamela.

His throat tightened as he stood nearby, watching the EMTs work quietly around Kara, calming her. Whoever had hit her had meant to break her nose. Trying to suppress his rage, he knew he had plenty to do when they took Kara out of here. Already, a forensics team was on their way here. If they could look at tire treads or boot prints in the parking lot or anything else, they might get a lead on her attacker. But Cade wasn't holding out much hope of that because the recent thunderstorm had probably washed them away. But inside the building, the team might be able to lift fingerprints or DNA from her attacker.

Cade knew he'd be busy well into the evening. When he got done with his investigation here, working with the photographer and forensics team, he'd drive to the hospital and take Kara's statement. His weekend going fishing wasn't going to happen now, but he wasn't disappointed about it.

His spirits lifted as he thought of being able to see Kara alone. *At last...a dream come true.* Cade was scared because the lawman in him knew this break-in could either be a one-time thing or worse, it could be someone after Kara. That grim knowledge made him want to find some clue that would lead to the attacker's capture. Maybe when he talked to Kara, he'd find out more.

IT WAS NEARLY nine p.m. when Cade finished up with the investigation team at the school. The weather was humid from the Gulf air smothering the area after a second line of thunderstorms rolled through in the early evening hours. He talked to the ER physician who had seen Kara; she wanted her to stay overnight for observation. Kara had sustained a mild, level two concussion. Clamping down on his anger toward her unknown attacker, Cade took the exit stairs up to the second floor of the three-story hospital where she was being treated.

Because it was after visiting hours, he checked in at the nurse's station to get directions to Kara's room and give them his name and badge number. No one was allowed on the floors after eight p.m. without good reason and it was a good security measure.

Cade was glad to see Kara had a corner room, a private one. The door was closed so he knocked lightly before entering, not wanting to scare the hell out of her. The TV was on with the volume turned low. He walked through the outer area where the bathroom was located and halted at the second entrance. Kara had heard him and was sitting up in bed, wearing a light blue gown, the covers pooled around her waist.

"Hey," Cade called softly, removing his Stetson, "sorry to be so late getting here. How are you feeling?" Hungrily, he scanned her shadowed features, all the lights off except for the TV.

"Hi," she said, her voice rough. Clearing it, she said, "That's okay. Come on in, Cade." She gestured to a nearby chair on the left side of her bed. Picking up the remote, she turned off the

TV. "Go ahead and flip on some lights," she told him.

Nodding, he pushed one switch on, the lights farthest from her bed. Getting a good look at Kara's face, he saw her left eye had swollen shut and the surrounding flesh a deep purple-bluish color. She had a chemical ice pack in her hand that she'd been putting on it.

"Do you have a headache?" he asked, pulling up the chair and setting his tablet on the edge of the mattress near him.

"I did. The nurses gave me some ibuprofen earlier. It really helped reduce the swelling around this eye." She grimaced, giving him a worried look. "I look awful. I saw myself in the mirror when I went to the bathroom earlier."

Her hair was mussed and in need of a good brushing. His fingers itched to pick up that brush on the bed stand and do just that, but it was out of the question. That would be a highly intimate gesture and Cade knew it. "Well hey," he teased, giving her a slight smile as he sat down, "give it a week or two and you won't have that black eye any more. How's that nose of yours feeling?"

She sat back on her bed that had been raised, stuffing the pillows around her back and relaxing. "The doctor said that horrible breaking sound I heard in my head was the bone breaking. It sounded much worse than the break itself." She gently touched her swollen nose. "It's fractured, but the good news is there won't be any surgery, thank goodness."

"Good," he said, opening up his tablet, getting ready to use it for his report. "Did you get to see your mom earlier?"

"Yes. She was shocked that I was attacked. I told her I was fine, which was a lie. I just didn't want her to worry. She believed me. I told her I'd call her tomorrow morning after the doctor released me from the hospital."

"What about your father?"

"He was in Houston for a conference. Mom called him immediately after she talked to me and said I was going to be fine. I guess he didn't believe her and he's flying home right now. He's supposed to arrive soon." Looking away for a moment, she admitted distastefully, "I don't really like seeing him these days."

Leaning over, Cade set his Stetson on the bed stand. He heard the pain in her voice. "When I was around, I remember that you never wanted to go home at night after school."

She tilted her chin, studying him in the low light. "We don't get along. We've never seen eye-to-eye on anything, and I hated his efforts to control me." She pushed her damp palms against the light blue bedspread. "Probably sounds awful, but that's the way it is."

"Your father isn't exactly a warm, fuzzy person, Kara."

"No, and I'm the softy in the family," she said, her lips lifting a little. "He's always called me 'marshmallow,' and it was never said nicely, believe me."

He saw the weariness in her shadowed blue gaze as Kara picked nervously at a loose thread she'd found on the bedspread. Cade knew she was shy by nature and rarely made eye contact with anyone—even him. It looked like some things about her hadn't changed.

"But the kids you teach and have in day care love that side of you," he said gruffly. She lifted her head, and he saw the tears swimming in her eyes. She swallowed several times, battling them back.

"You say the nicest things, Cade. I wish…," and she opened her hands, leaning back against the pillows, "I wish we could have known one another better back in school. I knew you would understand how I felt now."

"Things were different then, Kara. I was from the wrong side of the tracks and your father didn't want white trash around you." He saw pain come to her eyes and instantly regretted his harsh comment.

"No one should ever be told they're white trash. He was wrong to do it then and now."

"He hates anyone who doesn't look like him, and who isn't as rich as he is," she muttered angrily, shaking her head, giving him an apologetic look. "I've never seen anyone as prejudiced as he is."

Cade wanted to get off that topic. "The only

thing we can change, Kara, is the present and ourselves."

She sighed. "You're right. When you stood in the entrance of the day care center, I didn't realize it was you until I looked closer at your eyes and mouth. Getting away from Clayton has done you good. You look great, Cade."

"Thanks." How badly he wanted to get personal with her. It was a selfish desire on his part and Cade knew he had other reasons for being here. "Life has a way of shaping or reshaping us." He held up his tablet. "Are you up for me taking a report on what happened to you?"

"I can't sleep. My mind and emotions are a jumble," she admitted. "Go ahead and ask me your questions for my statement."

"You'll feel better tomorrow morning," he reassured her, making a few touches on the screen. There was a warm light glowing in Kara's eyes, and Cade tried to tell himself it was his crazy-assed imagination at work. Getting down to business, he asked her exactly what had happened at the day care center.

When Kara finished her story, she added, "I have no idea who that man was."

"Would you have time to look at some photos? Your assailant might have a criminal record. I'm hoping forensics can find a good set of fingerprints from him at the day care center."

"Sure, I'll go with you and try to identify him. But is the sheriff's department open on Saturday?"

"Absolutely. Crime stopping doesn't take a holiday—we have three shifts, seven days a week. I think we can handle your visit to identify this dude, if possible."

"Will you be there?"

He heard the quiet strain in her tone and realized she was still terrorized. "It's my case, so I'll be there."

"I'm so glad…" Giving him a distraught look, she added, her voice a hoarse whisper, "I have this horrible feeling that he's still around. I can feel him nearby, Cade."

Brow furrowing, Cade heard the fear in her whisper. "You can feel him nearby?"

Shrugging, she said, "My mom is very psychic and I get it from her. My feelings have saved me from a lot of trouble, and once I avoided an accident by listening to them. I know this sounds crazy—"

"No, it doesn't. When I was in combat over in Afghanistan, there were times I had only a raw, primitive knowing that saved my butt. I'm not going to make fun of your knowing, Kara." At that moment, the hair on his neck stood up. Cade knew it was the sign of a threat and he snapped his gaze toward the doorway.

Jud Knight, dressed in a designer, blue pin-striped business suit, halted in the entrance, his narrowed gaze settling on his daughter.

"Kara," he demanded, "Are you all right?"

Cade said nothing, remaining silent, watching the man enter the room like he was a king. Every instinct in him wanted to throw Knight out of the room as he came and sat down on the edge of Kara's bed, his hands lightly framing his daughter's swollen face.

"I-I'm fine, Father, really," Kara pulled away, wanting to avoid any contact with him.

"How did this happen?" he asked, his voice rising. "Tell me everything."

Kara scooted back against the bed, wrapping her arms across her body. She told him what had happened in as few words as possible.

Cade saw Knight's face grow black with rage as he continued to study his daughter.

"I don't know him, Father. I was telling Deputy Patterson earlier about it. I gave him a full description of the man."

Knight got to his feet, glaring across the bed at Cade. "What are you doing about this, Deputy?"

"Ms. Knight is coming tomorrow to look through mug shots at the sheriff's office. By that time, my forensics team should have collected all the evidence that they could find resulting from the assault. And maybe some fingerprints left behind, if we get lucky."

Knight's fists knotted, standing tensely, looking between his daughter and the deputy. "He could have killed her!"

Cade was used to this man's drama tactics.

"But he didn't. Your daughter fought back and saved herself."

"No thanks to you and your law enforcement," Knight ground out.

Ruffled, but hiding it with his game face, Cade stared at the man whose arrogance dripped off him. His chin was thrust forward, his hands curling into fists. He wasn't going to verbally spar with Knight because he saw how stricken Kara was beginning to look because of her father's nasty reaction toward him.

"Father, I've had enough anger for one day," Kara said abruptly. "I'm fine. You can leave now."

"Your mother said you'd be released from this hospital tomorrow morning?"

Wearily she replied, "Yes."

"Then you need to come home and stay with us at the ranch after this attack." He lifted his index finger, shaking it in her general direction. "We built you a small house on the ranch years ago. It's ready for you to move in and make it your home. You'll be safe there, Kara. No one will beat you up like this goon did at the day care center. It's time you returned to us and learned how to run the ranch. Someday, you'll be a foreman. You need to quit this stupid Delos charity job and come home. That's all there is to it."

Cade saw Kara's eyes widen, and even her swollen one opened wider for a moment.

"I've heard this from you before, Father. I'm not quitting my Delos job and I'm not moving back to the ranch. I made that clear a long time ago. Nothing has changed."

Cade saw Knight's mouth tighten. He silently applauded her for taking charge and not allowing the bastard to run her over as he had when she was still under age.

"Now listen here, young lady—"

"Mr. Knight," Cade said in a firm, authoritative voice, slowly unwinding from the chair, "your daughter has been through a lot today and she's traumatized. I'd like to suggest we leave her to rest for now. I'm sure you can hold this type of conversation for a later date when she's gotten some rest and feels better."

Knight glared at him, his jaw jutting out, as he considered the suggestion.

"Go home, Father. When I'm released tomorrow I'm going back to my house to clean up. Then, Deputy Patterson is going to drive me to the Kenedy County Sheriff's Department to look at mug shots to see if I can identify the guy who did this to me. I won't be going out to the ranch for any reason."

Her jaw was set and Cade smiled inwardly. Kara might look soft, but she had her father's stubborn chin and a backbone of steel when she chose to use it. Father and daughter stared at one another like two pit bulls gauging each other's strength. There was no real love between these two. Cade felt sad for Kara because right now, she needed to feel loved and safe. Jud Knight was clearly incapable of either.

"Okay," Knight muttered, displeased. "But if you need anything you let me know, understand?"

"You'll be the first to know," Kara said. "Thanks for dropping by."

Cade wondered how often she'd said those same words to Knight. There wasn't a hint of parental love in the man's face for his daughter. That raked Cade's emotions the wrong way. If anything, Kara needed to be comforted right now and God help him, he wanted to be the man to do just that.

"You must call us tomorrow morning after you leave the hospital. I want to know how you're doing, Kara."

"I will. Goodnight, Father."

Cade held the man's hard look in his direction. He could see Jud wanted to say something to him, but had second thoughts. Knight turned on his heel and stormed out of the room. He couldn't even kiss his daughter or hug her goodbye? Was this how Kara had lived for eighteen years under his roof? The thought chilled Cade. Now he was seeing her family dynamics up close and personal. It left a very bitter taste in his mouth. He knew Pamela Knight. She was the soul of kindness and had passed it on to her daughter. It was a good thing her mother was there for her. Cade could see the devastation in Kara's eyes from that confrontation with her brutal, unfeeling father.

The room became silent once more.

"I'm sorry you had to see that," Kara whispered, giving him a look of regret.

"Has he always been that way with you?"

"I'm afraid so." She struggled and managed a weak smile. "He often told me the only way marshmallows—that was me—got toughened up was to treat them like they were in boot camp."

He fought down his disgust for Kara's sake and walked over to her bed. Gently, he asked, "Is there anything I can get you before I leave?"

"Could you close the door for a moment, Cade, please? I need to share something with you."

Surprised by her request, but keeping his game face on, Cade shut the door. What was this all about? As he turned, he brought over the nearby chair and sat beside her bed. He knew he was tall and sometimes looked threatening to many people with his uniform on, so Cade sat down. "What's going on?"

She moved her hand nervously across the front of her gown. "Cade, would you...could you stay with me tonight? Here?" Her voice grew strained. "One of the nurses told me earlier they could roll another bed in here because it's such a large room. You could guard me just for tonight, couldn't you? Because I feel like this animal wants to kidnap me or do something awful to me if he catches me again..."

CHAPTER 3

C ADE TRIED TO hide his surprise, but his heart rose for a moment, sensing there was hope that he could, in fact, be the man to support her. He reminded himself that Kara's tentative request wasn't about intimacy—she was simply terrified and saw him as protection. He was, after all, a deputy sheriff. Trying to tamp down his need for her on a personal level, keeping all his rising hopes at bay, he rasped, "Yes, I can do that."

"Are you sure?"

"I'm finished with my shift. I'm on overtime right now because of your case. If you feel this perp is still around, I'll stay and bunk in with you so you can get a decent night's sleep here."

She offered a thin smile. "No one sleeps well in a hospital."

Unable to resist a grin, Cade got up and rolled his shoulders to get rid of the tension.

"That's true. I'm going to go talk to the night staff, Kara. I'll be right back."

She nodded, relieved. He resisted the urge to reach down and gently pull her into his arms. He knew this was what Kara needed more than anything—just to be held by another human being. This wasn't about sex. It was about care of another person when they needed it the most.

He had noticed how she tended to hold herself with her arms wrapped around her waist. He was adept at reading facial expressions, body language, and tonal variations, and this one gesture told him that Kara felt raw and unprotected, believing the world around her was threatening. Holding herself like that also meant she was struggling to keep her emotions at bay.

Cade wanted to give her what she really needed, but couldn't. It would be too easily interpreted as an intimate gesture, crossing a line that should never be crossed between a law enforcement officer and someone being assisted.

Moving quietly out of the room, Cade went over to the nurse's station, where two women were on duty for the overnight shift. His emotions were still raw thinking about Knight's behavior toward his daughter and Kara's strong intuitive belief that the perp was still around.

He knew the hospital had set up excellent security measures because he'd worked with the staff six months earlier, putting them into place. Out of habit, Cade's gaze swept the quiet, nearly darkened area. The main double doors to the ward were closed and he tested them to make sure they were secure. They were.

He introduced himself to the two new nurses who had recently come on for their shift and shared with them Kara's unease. Both older women gave him a look of understanding.

"It could be she's still in shock," one suggested.

"I know Kara," the blonde nurse spoke up. "She's very psychic—almost scarily so. She warned me one time that my son, Timmy, should be careful where he rode his bike the next day. Darned if she wasn't right. Timmy had an accident and ended up with a broken toe. I believe if that's how Kara feels, Deputy Patterson, you'd best believe her."

The other nurse grimaced. "Well, we need to stay especially alert tonight, then, Olivia."

"I'll get up and make rounds about once an hour," Cade reassured them. "And if you hear, or see, or sense anything out of the ordinary, come and get me in Ms. Knight's room."

"Oh, good," Olivia said. "We don't need a monster like that trying to get into our hospital."

"No," Cade agreed, "we don't. Can you dial me security, Olivia? I want to talk to whoever's in charge of the night shift. I want them on their toes about this situation, too."

By the time the two nurses rolled the visitor's bed into Kara's room, she was lying down. In no time, they had the bed prepared for Cade. After they left, he made sure the door was slightly ajar, wanting to acquaint himself with the normal sounds within the ward. He turned and saw that Kara had opened one eye. The other was swollen shut, and he wished he could take away her pain.

"I'm going to sleep," she mumbled. "I feel so tired."

He walked over, pulling the covers up to where her hands rested at her waist. Cade had to struggle not to get too personal with her. "Stay warm, okay? I'll be up and down all night, so don't be alarmed if you wake up and hear me moving around. The doors to this ward are locked. Security downstairs knows about the potential threat, so everyone here is on high alert." He slipped the bedspread into her waiting hands. "You'll be okay, Kara. Get some sleep. I'll see you in the morning."

Cade watched as one corner of her mouth hooked faintly upward. She was lying on her right side, the puffiness and swelling on the left side of her cheek making it impossible to take any other position unless she slept on her back or belly, which he doubted she would do under the circumstances. Her hair, even in the low light, gleamed with amber threads among the sable strands. An ache began in his chest and, without thinking, he touched her hair as he watched her quickly drop asleep. Right now, Kara was frightened and in need of a sense of protection.

Cade could give her that. He wanted to do that for her.

Another part of him was filled with deep anger as he silently moved away from her bed. Flexing his hands, he wanted to plant a fist into Jud Knight's smug face. Now he was getting a taste of what Kara had lived with daily as she grew up in that dysfunctional ranch family. How Pamela Knight could love someone like him was beyond Cade's understanding.

His bed was about six feet away from Kara's, and he loosened his belt, placing his holster and pistol on a rolling tray that sat nearby. He would keep his boots and clothes on in case there was trouble. All he'd have to do was grab his weapon.

There was a sliver of light cascading through the partly cracked door, enough for him to see easily, should he have to get up and maneuver around Kara's bed. Glancing over at her shadowy form, he saw how the blankets, pulled up to her shoulders, delicately outlined her body. Hungrily, he noted the curves and valleys of her silhouetted profile, appreciating her flared hips and the outline of her long, slender legs.

Kara had been a skinny little girl in grade school and had started to fill out in junior high. By high school, she was a beautiful, but untouchable young woman, bursting with promise. As Cade lay down on his back, punching the pillow into place beneath his head. In grade school, Kara had always loved to put her long brown hair into a set of braids. Cade remembered that every day, she would wrap a velvety, colorful ribbon around the end of each one.

Closing his eyes, sliding his hands behind his head, he felt his body begin to relax for the first time today. Cade had learned to tell by the color of the ribbons how Kara was feeling. He'd never talked to her, but observed her from afar.

When she seemed very sad, she seemed to choose blue ribbons. Had that been a day when her father had taken her to task by deriding her and making her feel bad about herself? Verbal abuse by calling her a "marshmallow?" Or something worse and shaming?

On the days she wore red ribbons, she was ebullient, smiling, laughing, and more outgoing. Were those days when her father was out of town, perhaps away from the ranch, giving her respite from his daily dark shadow?

He had so many questions for Kara. The shock of seeing her suddenly after so many years was still flowing powerfully through him. Cade was sure it was going to take time before he got over the jolt of that unexpected meeting. Dreaming about Kara was one thing. Seeing her in person was, *Wow!*

Sighing, Cade felt the first evidence of exhaustion, which had been stalking him since Kara's assault. He had one ear keyed to Kara's soft breathing while the other ear registered the noises outside the room at the nurse's station.

And miraculously, Kara was only six feet away from him. Six feet! He knew that for the next week, Kara would be feeling pretty much out of balance, dealing with the shock of being attacked. That black eye and her swollen cheek would be painful. He wondered if she'd try to teach school on Monday. Knowing Kara, she probably would.

If nothing else, she was a devoted, passionate person and the Delos Home School had been her vision from what his mother had told him. Kara had manifested it on behalf of the people of Clayton. At least, that was the word from his mother, who thought she was truly an angel come to earth to help the less fortunate.

When the sheriff's department hired him a year ago, after graduation, he was told all about the local businesses. His heart had leapt when his supervisor mentioned that Kara Knight was the administrator for the Delos Home School, and from that moment on, Cade had fought going to see her. He couldn't face the possibility of rejection, and he figured she was probably married or had a boyfriend.

That was another shock—to discover she had neither in her life. Did it leave room for him? For them to explore the possibilities? He'd loved her from afar from the moment they'd met in the first grade until he'd graduated from high school and gone into the Marine Corps. And even then, Kara had stayed in his heart, though she'd never realized it.

Because of his black ops background, Cade didn't allow himself to sleep deeply. He automatically woke up an hour later and lay there, waiting and listening. Maybe by morning, Kara would feel better. It bothered the hell out of him knowing her assailant might still be around, waiting, watching. Why had he attacked her? Was it a robbery gone wrong? Had the perp thought everyone was gone from the school and been surprised by Kara being there?

There were a lot of robberies around Clayton, mainly because it sat so close to the Mexico border. Undocumented workers coming through weren't likely to steal from Clayton, but the Gomez drug cartel was right across the Rio Grande in McCall, Texas, which was only thirty miles away from Clayton. The town suffered because a main, less-used highway, stretched between it and Sarita, a favorite of drug soldiers trying to bring drugs into the U.S. He had no answers, just a lot of damned, unanswered questions. Kara was probably collateral damage on a robbery gone wrong. From the description she gave of her assaulter, Cade was fairly sure he worked for the Gomez cartel.

KARA FELT DRUGGED when she awoke the next morning. The clock on the opposite wall read nine a.m. With a start, she sat up. She'd never slept so late before! The door was closed and she saw the other bed was rumpled, but Cade was gone. She touched her swollen cheek and to her relief, it felt slightly better, not as fiery. The throbbing had reduced a lot.

Dragging herself out of bed, she put on the pair of socks the nurses had given her and went to the bathroom. Her bloody clothes had been placed in a plastic bag and she had nothing else to wear. She wrinkled her nose, smelling the dried blood on her white blouse as she opened it up. The blue hospital gown was chafing her sensitive skin and she wished for the silk, knee-length nightgown she wore at home.

After taking a shower, Kara reluctantly pulled on her clothes from yesterday. She wished she could hide the blood all across the front of her blouse, but she couldn't. She did feel better after getting her teeth brushed, her hair washed, and taking a good, hot shower.

She decided she looked pretty ugly as she studied the left side of her face, but at least now her eye wasn't completely swollen shut and she could see out of it. She noted how pale her skin was as she used the dryer on her hair.

Her heart turned to Cade. How badly she had yearned for him to come over and wrap his strong, caring arms around her yesterday. She swore she saw longing in his expression, but she was afraid to trust her inner knowing. She'd been so shocked by the assault that she was beginning to question her own intuition. And her sense that the man who assaulted her was still hunting for her, was probably only her overactive imagination because her emotions overrode her normal logic and common sense yesterday. Cade had taken her at her word and for that, Kara would be forever grateful to him for remaining with her so she could sleep deeply last night.

Just as she was stepping out of the bathroom, she spied Cade entering her room. He hadn't shaved and the darkness of his beard gave a dangerous, masculine cast to his face.

But that didn't scare Kara. Instead, her whole body responded purely on a feminine level to him, woman-to-man. His black Stetson sat low on his brow and he looked official, on guard, his gaze locking and holding with hers.

She, on the other hand, felt disheveled.

"Hey," she said, "is everything okay out there?"

Cade halted, quickly perusing her from head to toe, then returning to her eyes. "Everything's quiet. How are you feeling, Kara?"

Her skin flushed beneath that gruff question. Yes, her dormant sexual self was coming online. He wasn't trying to hide behind that game face he wore last night. This morning, for whatever reason, Cade looked vulnerable, just as she desperately needed him to be with her.

"Better. My cheek isn't as swollen," she said,

barely touching the area with her fingertips.

"Are you in pain?"

That was a loaded question and one she didn't want to answer here. Maybe never. "No. There's just a bit of throbbing, but not much. Not like yesterday." Managing a slight upturn of her lips, she added, "At least I can see out of my left eye now. It's opened up a little. That's progress in my book."

"Good," he murmured. "In another day, it will look even better. The worst is over."

"Says the guy who's had a black eye before. Right?" she teased, seeking the warmth entering his expression. What would it be like to be bold enough to walk up to Cade, wrap her arms around his neck, and draw him against her? The thought was filled with possibilities and Kara didn't try to dodge the feelings that were growing by the second for him.

The man was a babe magnet, no question. His youthful features had filled out, his body had matured, and to her, he looked beautiful in a very alpha male sort of way. Even now, she could feel a twinge deep in her body, a signal that it too, was interested in him on more than a casual friendship level.

A sour grin tugged at Cade's mouth over her question. "Yeah, I've had a few black eyes in my day. I'm practically an expert on them. Are you ready to sign out? Your doctor just came in to make her rounds and she wants to see you. I can drive you to your home afterward if you'd like."

"Yes, I would appreciate that. Thank you, Cade."

Cade became serious. "What I'd like to do, if you feel up to it, Kara, is to get you home so you can change your clothes and get something to eat. Then, I'll drive you to Sarita to see if you can identify your assailant from our identification database. Afterwards, I'll take you to the Delos Home School so that you can pick up your car and go home. How does that sound?"

"Wonderful."

"Are you dizzy at all? You were yesterday."

Shaking her head, she said, "No, I feel much better today."

"It's the fine care you got here by the folks at the hospital," he agreed.

No. That wasn't the total reason, although the hospital staff had been caring and wonderful. The other reason was Cade. But Kara wasn't about to tell him that. She had no idea how he'd react to her honesty. "Everyone has been very kind to me here."

"They're like that. I see you slept long and hard."

"How much sleep did you get?"

Cade shrugged those capable shoulders of his, her fingers itched to slide across them and feel the power within him.

"Enough to keep operating today. I'm sure tonight I'll crash and burn in my own bed."

"You live in Sarita?"

"Yes."

Kara wished he lived in Clayton. There was twenty miles between the two largest towns in the county.

Studying her, Cade asked, "Are you still feeling that the perp is around this morning?"

Relieved that he respected her intuition, Kara said, "Yes, and I wish I didn't, but I do feel it…feel him. And I feel so violated…" Giving him a rueful look, she added, "Sometimes, I think I'm making it up because of getting hit yesterday. Normally, my intuition is good."

"I trust what you know, so don't worry about it. And it's all the more reason for me to take you home."

She gave him a grateful look. "I'm so glad you're here, Cade. I trust you. I always did."

"Well," he said, giving her a reassuring look, "you keep doing that. I'll keep you safe."

"You have no idea how good that feels to me." She drowned in his warming gaze, seeing his mouth relax, feeling that same invisible warmth embracing her.

"Now," he said lightly, "that I'm back in your life, I'd like to at least be there for you when you need help."

KARA GASPED AS Cade pulled the cruiser into

the red brick driveway next to her one-story home. "My front door is open!" she cried, giving Cade a frightened look. "I always lock my doors! Someone has broken into my home. Oh, no!"

Cade parked and frowned. "Does anyone else have a key to your place?"

"No, no one." She tried to calm herself.

"Stay here," he told her grimly, unsnapping the nylon safety strap across his revolver. He called the Sarita dispatcher for back up, another cruiser to lend him help, if he needed it. Turning to her, he said, "I need to clear your home first and make sure someone isn't still in there. Don't leave this cruiser, Kara. Lock the doors when I leave."

Giving a jerky nod, her hand against her throat, heart banging away in her chest, she watched Cade move lithely, tension in his body, his gun drawn as he walked past the hedges to the front door. She knew without a doubt it was the same man who had accosted her at the school. Terror leaked into her veins and she sat rigid as Cade disappeared inside. Her intuition hadn't been wrong after all.

Cade couldn't be hurt! Her mind rebelled at that thought. What if her assailant was still in the house waiting for her to return home to finish her off?

Within ten minutes, Cade reappeared. He had his game face in place, his gun holstered, and his mouth set with cold determination. He climbed into the cruiser, giving her a regretful look. "Someone has torn the hell out of your place. All the drawers in your bedroom and office have been pulled out and the contents strewn all over the floor. I'm sorry."

Gasping, her hand against her lips, she stared at him. Finally, her voice hoarse, she asked, "Who could be doing this to me? And why?"

Shaking his head, he muttered, "I don't know, but I have to call this in, Kara. I need to get the forensics team out here. I don't want you inside your home until they've gotten here."

He pressed the button on his shoulder radio, calling Sarita dispatch, and gave them the information.

Her stomach knotted and her hands grew cold and damp in her lap. She felt as if her whole world had just been shattered. Her small yellow stucco house with white shutters around each window had been her refuge, her oasis, her haven since graduating from Texas A&M University at twenty-two. She'd used her one-bedroom house to create her vision for the Delos Home School and for the many poor children of Clayton. All her dreams, except one, had been born and taken root in this cozy little house that made her feel safe.

Staring at the opened door, she felt nauseous. It looked as if someone had pried her door open and broken it. Some of the wood was splintered and the pieces of wood were lying around the porch.

Swallowing several times, Kara did what she did when she was a child; forced back the tears because her father hated seeing her or her mother cry. Never had she been so glad to turn eighteen and be free of her father's iron grip. Now she could breathe and have a life of her own, on her terms. She had a vision and she'd made it a reality. Her little house sat in the middle of the block of a quiet neighborhood in the "Latino Quarter," as it was called by Clayton residents.

She vaguely listened to Cade speaking to the radio dispatcher over what to do about her house. She was grateful to be this close to him, to draw in his male scent that continued to awaken her dormant desires. If only—if only they could have some personal quiet time together. Kara wondered when her life would stop tumbling out of control.

"Kara?"

She lifted her chin, meeting Cade's concerned gaze. "Yes?"

"Did you hear me?"

"No… sorry…I was somewhere else." She saw his eyes lose their concern, replaced by an intimate look of understanding that made her feel safer.

"Forensics will be here shortly. Another deputy, Burt Larson, is also on his way over here to relieve me. One of the forensics people can take you inside your house to pack a bag with whatever you might need after they make a primary inspection of your home."

"Maybe my teacher friends, Blaine or Molly, would let me stay with one of them," she said.

"I don't think so, Kara." He reached out and his hand covered hers for a brief moment. "It could endanger your friends."

She groaned. "You're right…"

Gesturing to the house, he said, "Whoever did this is still out there prowling around. What if he follows us to one of your girlfriend's homes? He might attack you there and you'd possibly put your friend in danger, too."

Her stomach sank. "I don't want my friends harmed in this," she murmured, touching her brow. "I don't have a lot of money, Cade. I can't afford a hotel." More grimly, she added, "And I'm not going to my father's ranch. I refuse to go there, Cade. I just won't do it."

"It would be the safest place for you right now, Kara," he said, surprising her.

"Not a chance," she muttered. "I escaped him when I was eighteen and I'm not going to do a repeat. I visit my mom there sometimes, but usually, she drives into Clayton and we have lunch together and catch up with one another."

"It's that bad?" He searched her eyes, seeing anguish in them. The way she pursed her lips told him the question was causing her pain.

"It's that bad."

"I'm sorry." Cade rested his hands on the

steering wheel, gazing around, his mouth set in thought.

The silence in the cruiser was nearly unbearable to Kara. Opening her hands, she said, "Cade, I have an idea that you'll probably dislike as much as me going to stay at my father's ranch until we can catch this guy."

"What?" he asked, looking over at her.

Taking a deep breath, Kara asked, "Could I stay with you at your home in Sarita for just a little while?"

Cade froze inwardly for a moment, stunned by her request. "Well," he stumbled, "I—"

"We know one another," she pleaded, her voice hoarse. "I'd be safe there, Cade. It wouldn't be for long. I'm sure this guy will be found and I can get back to my life. Please? Think about it? I could drive to and from your house to the school every morning. I promise, I wouldn't be a bad house guest. I don't want to go back to my father's ranch. I don't have the money for a hotel. And I don't want to put my friends at risk, either."

Opening his hands on the steering wheel, he said, "This is something I'd have to clear with my boss first, Kara."

She stared at him, hands clasped tightly. "Then, you'd think about it?"

"Yeah, I have no problem with it personally, but I'm law enforcement, and this could be crossing lines that my boss may not allow. I'd have to clear it with him first. If I do get permission, I think under the circumstances it's the best answer for you short term. I have a three-bedroom, single-story house. I'd give you the master bedroom because it has an adjoining bathroom. I'm a pretty decent cook, so I wouldn't poison you," and he gave her a boyish grin. "If I get permission, you could stay there with me and be safe until we can apprehend this perp."

Safe! Cade wasn't safe to her heart or her body, but she didn't have the guts to point that out to him. He'd only touched her once. His large, roughened hand comforting her. "That would be wonderful. I have to go to work five days a week, Monday through Friday."

"We can possibly put a deputy with you at the school and you'd get around-the-clock protection until we can find this guy. I'll ask my boss about it."

"I understand, Cade. And I'm grateful you'd allow me to come and stay with you under the circumstances."

"Well," he said grimly, "you need to stay somewhere until this blows over."

"I also need to make a call to Delos Charities in Alexandria, Virginia. They've instituted a new security plan and I have to report my mugging at the school. From talking with Alexa, one of the executives there, I know that Mission Planning would take my report and if warranted, send out one or more security contractors who work for Artemis, their in-house security firm, who protects their charity and the employees."

Brows raised, Cade said, "I didn't know that."

"Delos keeps Artemis a deep secret. But it's their way to protect all of us who work for them."

"Do you want to call them now? Because we have to wait here until the other deputy to arrives. Meanwhile, I can call my boss and see if he'll give you permission to stay at my home. Either way, I'll take you to look at those mug shots."

"Sounds good." She dug her cellphone out of her purse.

"I'll step out of the cruiser to make the call," he told her, opening the door.

Nodding, Kara whispered, "I hope you can get permission."

He hesitated, holding her gaze. "I do too. I'll know in a few minutes."

Never had Kara wanted something as badly as this. She knew she'd not sleep a wink if she was forced to stay in her house under the circumstances. The look in Cade's eyes had shown shock at first, but then, they'd grown tender and she couldn't translate what she saw, only felt. No question, he was protective of her and she needed that desperately right now. Putting that aside, she called Delos.

★

KARA HAD HER answer from Delos. It took another five minutes before Cade finished off his phone call and slid back into the cruiser. She held her breath because she couldn't discern what the answer was on Cade's face.

"The sheriff's approving it," he told her. "And you're not going to like the reason why."

"Tell me."

"He's doing it because you're Jud Knight's daughter." Holding up his hand when she started to protest, he added, "And he said if you didn't like the arrangement with me at my home, then you *had* to go to the ranch until this perp could be caught." His mouth quirked. "I guess I'm the lesser of two evils here, huh?"

"I'm pissed that your boss is doing it because I'm Jud Knight's daughter."

"Yeah, I figured you would be," Cade acknowledged, giving her a sour grin.

"I'm grateful that you'd open your home to me, Cade." She reached out, gripping his hand resting on his thigh. "Thank you...for everything. You have no idea how relieved I am."

"I'm glad to do it for you, Kara."

She saw the sincerity, the concern, in Cade's gaze. "I'm putting you out, Cade. I hate doing that. You have a life to live."

"Naw, you're an easy keeper, Ms. Knight. Don't worry about it." His mouth was sculpted, strong. And yet, Kara could see the kindness in it when the corners lifted slightly. She felt heat boiling within her, as if she were waking up from a nightmare and moving into a heated fantasy dream. How many times as a teen had she dreamed about Cade? Too many to count. Even more astounding, he was opening his home up to her.

"Because I'm a stray?" she teased back.

Giving her a deep laugh, Cade held her sparkling eyes that now contained a bit more life in them. "You've never been a stray, Kara. You were homecoming queen and a popular cheerleader in high school."

Losing her smile, she whispered, "I hated being queen. My father told the principal to choose me or he wouldn't donate to the school like he always did on a yearly basis. As for being a cheerleader, I hated that too. I preferred the library or a lab to all that other stuff."

She saw the surprise flare in his eyes. Opening her hands, she said, "My father buys people. Surely you knew that, Cade."

"Yes, most people in Kenedy County know about your father's power. I always thought you enjoyed being a cheerleader. You sure looked like you did."

"I was too young and immature to fight him on it. He's tried to brainwash me with the fact we're worth millions and because of the money, I should have these experiences in high school."

Wrinkling her nose, she added distastefully, "I'm an introvert, Cade. I don't enjoy crowds or being the center of attention."

"I had always thought you were shy, Kara. But on the field, when I played football, you always looked happy cheerleading from the sidelines."

"It was all fake," she told him bitterly.

"Maybe so, but you were a terrific cheerleader," he insisted. "I would never have guessed."

"That's because my father was at every game. I didn't want him coming down there to the cheerleader area and trying to tell me what to do, how to smile, and all that crap." She saw his mouth widen, a glint of humor in his gaze.

"You're just full of surprises."

Snorting softly, Kara said in a pained tone, "No one knows what I went through. I felt more like a slave at home than anything else. I looked forward to going to school because it meant eight hours of freedom when my father wasn't around trying to control me. He did it all, Cade, telling me how to fix my hair, which cosmetics to use, or God help us all, choosing the clothes I had to wear."

He was shocked but simply said, "Sounds pretty suffocating."

"It was. I'll never go back to that ranch and stay with him. He wants me to learn the ranching business, but I refuse. He tried to bribe me by paying for my teaching degree at Texas A&M in exchange for coming back to learn how to be the foreman. When I got my degree, I told him I wasn't going to do it. I was twenty-two and an adult. I had other dreams I wanted to fulfill. And mostly, I was tired of fulfilling his expectations at a great cost to myself."

"What did he do then?"

"Got angry, yelled at me, embarrassed me in front of all my friends who were at graduation. He cut me off from my weekly check. I found myself destitute. Blaine let me live with her until I could get my life sorted out. I had already signed up with Delos Charities and they gave me the direction I was looking for. They wanted to build a school and day care center in Clayton and they needed a manager and a leader. Thanks to their generous monthly salary, I was able to put a down payment on my beautiful little house here."

"And you've been the administrator for the Delos Home School for the past five years?"

Nodding, she said, "Yes, and I love what I do, Cade. I feel good about myself, good about helping others. Teaching is all I ever wanted to do."

"You should always follow your heart, Kara. Things work out better when you do."

She sighed. "I know that now, more than ever. I have to call Delos again and tell them what happened and that I can stay with you," she said, digging into her purse. Wyatt Lockwood, who is the head of Mission Planning asked me to keep him in the loop, so I need to let him know."

"Go ahead," Cade said. "Burt probably won't get here for another ten minutes. We have time."

She punched in the Delos number on her phone. "And I can stay with you."

"Yes. I wouldn't want it any other way."

She looked straight at him. "Neither would I."

CHAPTER 4

C ADE SEEMED IMPRESSED with Artemis, the secret security firm operating within Delos Charities. Kara spoke at length with Wyatt Lockwood. At one point, when Wyatt found out she would be living with Cade until this issue blew over, he asked to speak with him. She sat there listening to the timbre of Cade's voice, and gratefully noted his quick smile and laughter every now and then as he spoke at length with Wyatt.

It made her feel happy knowing that Wyatt had previously been a Navy SEAL and that Cade was ex-military, too. It seemed to be a mutual admiration society between the two men, which was great as far as she was concerned.

Cade had just finished the phone call to Artemis when Deputy Burt Larson pulled up beside them in his cruiser. Right behind him was the forensic team's white van with a blue center stripe on the vehicle. "The cavalry has arrived," he said, his fingers brushing hers as he passed the phone back to her.

"Can I gather a few things in one of my pieces of luggage now?"

"Let's have forensics get in there first and give it a once over. Then, one of them can escort you through safe areas so you won't accidentally compromise their investigation."

"Okay, that makes a lot of sense," she said, stuffing the phone into her purse.

Cade climbed out, coming around to open her door.

"You don't have to do that," Kara protested.

He looked amused. "But I want to." Stepping back, he held out his hand toward her, looking for an excuse to touch her, even briefly.

She slipped her hand into his, relishing the quiet strength of his fingers around hers, feeling the roughness of his skin, her whole body going into overdrive from their delicious, unexpected contact. There was a glint in his eyes and she wanted, once more, to have quiet, uninterrupted time with Cade to catch up, to see how his life had unfolded thus far. So many questions and no time to ask them, at least not yet.

Kara got to meet Burt, who was in his mid-thirties, at least six feet tall, well built, intense, and alert. She found out he was happily married and had three young daughters. He shook her hand and she appreciated his courtly manners. The forensics team consisted of two women who also shook her hand. Within twenty minutes, they had escorted her into her house. Kara's heart sank as she saw the mess in her home. She wanted to cry. Her belongings were strewn across every room, her glass perfume bottle broken, swept off her antique sideboard, scattered in pieces across the oak floor. Gulping, she knew it could all be cleaned up and that while some things could not be salvaged, many others could. In no time, she gathered clothing, toiletries, and anything else she thought she might need.

It was hard to tell how long she would be gone from her home. Knowing she'd be safe with Cade made her feel better and fed her strength to get through this unfolding nightmare.

Curious, her seventy-year-old next door neighbor, Carolyn, came over to meet her outside. "Hey, Kara," she said, lifting up her cellphone, "I got somethin' that might help you and the deputies here."

She shook Cade's hand, introducing herself. Fiddling with her phone, she said to them, "Yesterday I saw this black pickup pull into your driveway, Kara. We have a neighborhood block watch around here and I didn't recognize it, so I took some photos." She gave them a pleased look. "Maybe this is the guy that tore up your house," and she turned the screen so Cade and Kara could look at it.

Kara gasped as she saw the man. "That's

him!" she cried, giving Cade a stricken look. "That's him! He's the one who attacked me at the school!"

Cade's eyes narrowed. "Great photo, Carolyn. You did good—very good!"

"Oh, Carolyn, these are so helpful!" Kara said, watching as Cade took the phone and then slid his finger through all the shots she'd taken of the intruder. He held it at an angle so she could see them as well. Throat tightening, she winced as she saw the same angry looking eyes. Fear trickled through her once more. The man could have killed her instead of merely breaking her nose.

"I didn't recognize him, Kara. He was new to our block." Carolyn's dark brown eyes twinkled. "I also got his license plate number. Take a look at the last photo, Deputy Patterson," she wriggled her finger toward her cellphone, another pleased look wreathing her wrinkled face.

Cade's mouth twitched as he studied the clear, close-up shot of the license plate. "You're a gem, Carolyn. Do you mind if I send these photos to the sheriff's department right now?"

"No, of course not. Do you know this guy?"

"No, ma'am, I don't. We'll put his face through our facial recognition software and hopefully it will come up with a hit. Thank you, again." He pulled out a business card from his pocket, handing it to Carolyn.

"And until he's caught," Kara said to Carolyn, "Deputy Patterson doesn't want me staying here at my home."

"Makes sense," Carolyn said. She lifted her chin and asked, "But how safe are the rest of us, Deputy?"

"I'll know more after we ID this perp," he told Carolyn. "Deputy Larson over there with the forensics team is going to take your report. He'll get your phone number too. Once we get back to headquarters, he'll call and keep you updated on any developments. My gut tells me someone's sent him after Kara but we don't know why yet. I think all you neighbors need to remain vigilant and alert, just in case. Call us immediately if you see anything out of place, or there's an unknown vehicle and driver casing your street."

"Oh," she drawled, "we'll do that for sure. There are always a lot of break-ins here because we live in Clayton. I'll contact my other neighborhood watch people on the block, send the photos I took to their email accounts, and we'll stay on guard."

Wincing over Carolyn's "wrong side of the tracks" comment, Kara knew it was because of her father's unbending prejudice against the poor and middle class of Clayton. These good, hardworking people were the backbone of the community and they struggled daily to keep their heads above water. Reaching out, she hugged Carolyn. "Thank you for all you've done. This is so helpful."

Cade smiled and handed the phone back to Carolyn. "You've just saved us a lot of time in trying to find this guy. Thank you."

"Well, the way I see it, if we don't look out for each other, we have nothing," Carolyn said.

KARA FELT SO much weight lift off her shoulders later at the Kenedy County Sheriff's Department. Cade had taken her into the busy building and then to his small, quiet office. There, Carolyn's emailed photos quickly identified her attacker. His name was Javier Fuentes, a known drug-runner with the Gomez drug cartel that operated out of the Mexican border town of Reynosa. This town was directly across the Rio Grande River from McAllen, Texas. The area was a hotbed of drug trafficking activity. Cade took her to a wall map, pointing out where the Mexican town was located along the border with Texas.

"Unfortunately," Cade told her, moving his index finger along Interstate 69 East out of Harlingen, Texas, "a lot of drug runners take this route. Outside of Raymondville, the interstate stops and drops to a two-lane highway, Route 77, which is where Clayton is located. They use 77 a lot to move drugs through this particular area because it's fairly unpopulated. Usually, it's a nighttime activity and they're pushing their cocaine, heroin, and marijuana along this route.

They can speed along at a hundred miles per hour with no other traffic in either direction. The whole of Kenedy County is owned ranchers, with a lot of pasture lands, small knolls, and trees here and there. There's no towns along this route, which is why they like to use it."

"You've got your hands full then," Kara said, studying the map, "because that highway goes straight through the middle of the county."

"Yes," Cade said. "It's a low population county and from a drug enforcement perspective, we are overwhelmed. The Gomez cartel is launching drones offshore from boats in the nearby Gulf. They remain close to the U.S. coastline and they're dropping bags of cocaine onto the beach. Drug soldiers like Fuentes wait at a pre-arranged point and retrieve the drone shipment. From there, they drive up Route 77 through Sarita and Rivera and then on to the larger cities east and north of them where the drugs are distributed."

"I didn't realize all of this was going on," she confessed, frowning.

"We work with the DEA, ATF, ICE, and the FBI, plus other law enforcement agencies like the Texas Rangers and the U.S. Border Patrol. We just don't have the manpower to handle all of this drug activity by ourselves and generally speaking, there's constant drug shipments brought in along the Gulf Coast of Texas."

"That's dangerous work, Cade."

"Police work always is. Let's get you home—I mean, to my home. You're looking tired, Kara."

"I guess I'm pretty stressed out over everything," she agreed. Earlier, she'd called Blaine and Molly, letting them know what had happened. They promised to go over and ensure that everything was clean at the school and ready to receive the children on Monday. Sophia Marquez, her assigned Artemis bodyguard, would meet her at the school on Monday as well. She was flying in from Alexandria, Virginia, the Delos HQ.

Wyatt had called her while Cade was driving her to Sarita. Sophia, he told her, had been an Army Ranger, one of the first women to make it through the grueling school and later, she joined the black ops Army group to be deployed to Afghanistan.

Wyatt had sent her the résumé and photo of the woman who would pose as the school's new assistant administrator. She had been born in Del Rio, Texas. Her parents had earned their green cards and eventually became American citizens. Sophia knew South Texas like the back of her hand, was aware of the drug problems in the area, and would be with Kara every day. She would follow Kara in her rental car to and from Cade's house, down to the Delos school in Clayton, and then follow her back to Sarita every afternoon. Knowing that Sophia was going to be there for her made Kara feel safer. Sophia had an impressive black ops background and Cade was very pleased with her résumé. He told Kara that for now, until they could figure out why she was being targeted, she would have twenty-four-hour-a-day guardians.

The drive from the sheriff's department to Cade's home on King Avenue was less than five minutes away. Sarita was a small town with roughly two-hundred and thirty-eight residents. Because this area got more rain than other parts of Texas, grass and trees flourished. As they approached Cade's home, she saw five pecan trees on both sides of his white stucco home with a red-tiled Spanish style roof. It was hot and humid in this area and the huge, large-limbed trees shaded the house from the blistering overhead rays.

She liked the white picket fence enclosing the lawn, front and sides of the house, as well as the screened-in wraparound porch. Flowers bloomed in window boxes, making the place look inviting. Everything was neat and well cared for. She'd always believed the outside of a house reflected the owner. Cade obviously took pride in his home.

"We're here," he murmured, pulling into the driveway and shutting off the cruiser.

"It's so pretty," she said, opening her own door and climbing out. Before she could retrieve her bag sitting on the rear seat, Cade had opened the door and pulled it out for her. She saw him give her an amused look once again, and she smiled a little, giving him a look of thanks. The red brick walk was bracketed by bright gold and yellow marigolds.

Cade moved ahead of her, pulling out the keys to his home from his pocket.

"Is this the proverbial yellow brick road?" she asked, gesturing to the flowers.

Grinning, he said, "Hey, I grew up with stories of Dorothy, Toto, and the Wizard of Oz. How about you?"

Coming to a halt a step below the wide brick porch entrance, she said, "I think you're giving a lot of yourself away by what you've created in this pretty yard."

"I don't mind you knowing who I am," he teased. Cade pushed open the heavy oak door. "Come on in, Kara." His voice dropped, his gaze holding hers. "Welcome home…"

She heard the sudden emotion in his thickened tone and it melted through her as nothing else ever had. Unable to meet his eyes, feeling suddenly tearful, wanting to rush into his arms to be held, she turned and stepped into his house. For an unknown reason, Cade put her in touch with all the emotions she tried to keep hidden. She'd grown up knowing that crying, looking weak, or appearing incapable was simply not accepted by her tyrannical father.

There was a wealth of natural light within the foyer, living room, and kitchen area, the open-concept design dazzling as she looked around.

There were two fifteen-foot Hawaiian corn plants, their shining green and red leaves giving the area colorful vibrancy. She loved house plants and spotted a massive prayer plant with white blooms in a mauve ceramic pot in the south corner of the room. She'd been in condos and apartments before where a bachelor lived. They all seemed to use dark colors, stark metal furniture, and no green plants. It always felt too masculine and sterile to Kara. She imagined that Cade's house would reflect that same kind of color and design, but it didn't. He was a man of many surprises, pleasant ones.

How little she knew of him—and how badly she wanted to know so much more!

This was not just a house. It was a home—a nest of the finest kind in Kara's opinion. The floors consisted of polished light brown pecan wood. Sunlight poured through the floor-to-ceiling windows, bouncing off it, creating a golden glow within the expansive area. There was a pale apricot color on the walls of the living room, a lavender wraparound sofa, paired with two similar overstuffed chairs nearby.

The rug was bright and colorful, swirls of rainbow shades. The white adobe fireplace was the centerpiece against a wall of caramel-colored Texas flagstone. She moved her fingers across the couch's tight nap of corduroy. Then, hearing the door close, she turned. Cade's full attention was on her.

"Does it meet with your expectations?" he smiled, hoping it had exceeded them. He walked over and stood near the end of the couch.

"This is a beautiful home, Cade." She moved her fingers across the nubby material. "And I love the color lavender. This whole living room just begs you to take your shoes off, get comfy, and just be."

"Good," he murmured. "That was the idea. Come on, I'll show you around."

She saw how pleased her words made him and wondered if he'd been nervous about showing her his home.

The open concept flowed into a stunning kitchen. Cade had selected a white marble counter with purple and black vein accents running through it. There was a six burner gas stove from the expensive Wolf brand. Only someone who really loved cooking would buy such a pricey item. Cade had said he wasn't too bad of a cook, but now she wondered if he'd been underplaying his talents. He was probably a gourmet chef in disguise and she smiled to herself about the possibility. Kara loved discovering all these hidden facets about him.

Walking ahead of Kara down a long, airy hallway, Cade opened the door on the right and stepped aside. "This is the master bedroom, but I want you to make it your own while you're here. Beyond it," and he gestured toward another door, "is the bathroom. I think you'll like what you see."

"I like it already," she said, moving into the room. There was a king-sized platform bed, a pale lavender chenille bedspread across it. All four sides of the bed were framed with a rolled, dark purple velvet that was just begging to be touched. What made her draw her breath and stunned her into momentary silence was what was behind the bed's purple velvet headboard.

Cade came and stood at her shoulder. "When I bought this house, I wanted some color in it. It took me a year to finish that mosaic panel. My mother is a watercolor artist and taught me a lot about the color wheel." He gave her a shy glance. "Funny, I just finished this panel a week ago and you're the first person to see the completed version."

He walked over to the left side of the mosaic panel, brushing his fingers over a corner area of the huge ten-foot-long panel. "Right here in this area is the last of the mosaic I laid and grouted. It's still a little bit damp, but it will dry out in a week. These are Texas bluebonnets," he said, studying the grout with the colorful blue, purple, and hints of pink of ceramic tile chips that he'd carefully inlaid to create a group of the famous state flower.

Pressing her hand against her heart, Kara stared at the mosaicked panel that rose from behind the purple velvet headboard. "This—" she began, her voice hushed, "is such a work of art, Cade. I mean," and she opened her hand, staring at the motif of a sloped hill of wildflowers that could be found in a Texas meadow, "it's incredible!" She saw his cheeks redden. He barely held her gaze, more boy than man in that moment over her emotional compliment. And then she realized that probably very, very few people had ever seen the beauty of his artwork.

"Thanks," he said awkwardly, rubbing his jaw. "The only other person who has seen it is my mom." Clearing his throat, his hand resting on the velvet headboard, he added, "My dad was a plumber by trade, but his hobby was creating mosaic panel art. My mother was always giving him suggestions on color because he was very poor at it and she's an artist in her spare time. They were a good team."

"I never knew your parents were so artistic."

"It was something they enjoyed doing. I grew up in Mom's small art room and then spent the rest of my time with my dad on weekends out in his garage where he had a table to make his mosaic art panels. Those were good times," he murmured.

"And now you're carrying that family tradition on," she said gently. "Has your mom given you help with the colors in your wildflower panel?"

He rocked back on the heels of his boots, stuffing his hands into his Levis. "Yes. As you know, she lives in Clayton, but I try to see her at least once a week, drop by for lunch, and catch up with how she's doing. When I told her I was working on the sketch, I brought it to her home for her to check out my panel idea. We spent hours talking about the different colors and how to really make it a visual feast of sorts for a person's eyes." He gave the panel a fond look, his voice going low. "There's a lot of my father and mother in this."

"Well," Kara said, her voice filled with emotion and pride, "that is the most beautiful panel I've ever seen. When I was younger, my father always took me and my mom on cruises and vacations to Europe. I got to see a lot of the insides of Gothic churches and their magnificent stained glass windows. He took us to fine art and sculpture museums, as well." She gestured to his artwork above the bed. "What you've done here, Cade, rivals those gorgeous stained glass windows of Europe. Your work just takes my breath away."

Again, his cheeks turned ruddy and he became suddenly shy, not the tough law enforcement officer she knew. Impacted by his vulnerability, Cade endeared himself to her even more than before.

"I'd never been outside the States," he admitted. "Except when I was in the Marine Corps. I've seen photos of those churches online. I don't really think my hobby attempts can be compared to them, Kara, but thanks for the compliment."

In that moment, she wanted to turn and wrap her arms around his shoulders and draw him to her. There was pain deep in his eyes and she could feel the hurt around him for a fleeting moment, guessing that it was about missing his father in his life. "I think your work is that good, Cade, and nothing's going to change my mind about it." She reached over, briefly touching his arm. "And even more important, you had a wonderful relationship with your dad. I'd give anything to have had one with mine but all he does is drive me away. I wish he weren't so controlling."

"Yeah, he's a piece of work, all right," was all Cade would say, trying to keep censure out of his voice. "Let's look at your bathroom, Kara. I think you'll like it," and he cupped her elbow, guiding her into it.

Cade's hand on her elbow was unexpected and she absorbed his light, monitoring touch. Her skin sizzled with pleasure. What would it be like to love this man fully and completely? Kara was not innocent to the world of relationships. Cade was stirring up her hormones, engaging her heart and the combination sent yearnings racing through her. He was so confident as a man, leashed power as a deputy. But here in the safety of his home, he allowed her to see another side to him—the unsure artist who had created an undeniable work of art.

Kara had never forgotten that his family had

been verbally maligned by her father too many times to count. A plumber was a necessary service provider in Jud's life, but he never respected Cade's father when he arrived at the ranch from time to time to fix plumbing issues. Kara had seen that lack of respect from her father toward everyone, especially from what he termed "the lower classes."

He'd been born with a silver spoon in his mouth and inherited the multi-million-dollar ranch from his father. Never had he worked to achieve an objective, so he couldn't relate to those with a dream, a vision, or just plain ambition.

Now, moving into the white tiled bathroom, she saw that the tiles repeated the colorful flowers found in Cade's mosaic. "Did you redo the bathroom floor?" she asked, as she pointed to the bluebonnets among the tiles.

"Yes." He shrugged a little. "My mother pointed it out. She said if I was going to make such a beautiful landscape, the bathroom should echo it in some way. She's the one who suggested I take up the pecan wood floor and lay down tile instead. When I was finished with my shift, I'd come home and work on it. We drove to Houston, to a well-known ceramic tile maker, and I bought the wildflower tiles to place among the white tiles I'd already purchased."

"How long did this take you?"

"Six months," he admitted. "Hey, I had to

teach myself how to lay tile and grout on a floor. And I was pulling overtime, so this became a half year's labor of love on my part."

"It's so pretty," Kara said, looking around. At one end of the room was a garden tub. It sat beneath an antique, stained glass window that sported geometric colors and could be opened to allow in fresh air. "Did your mom help you design your home?"

"Definitely. Couldn't have done it without her input," he admitted with a boyish grin, leaning against the opened door. "I needed a lot of help from her, believe me."

Kara appreciated the huge garden tub at the other end of the large, spacious bathroom. "When I walked into your home, I was so surprised. I was expecting a lot of dark colors, poorly lit rooms, and industrial type of furniture."

He lifted his brows. "Well, that's about right. After I purchased this house, I brought my mom over to give me some ideas. What I wanted is exactly what you just described. She told me to approach each room as a canvas to paint on, or in my case, a place where I would lay mosaic and grout the panel."

"She must be very proud of you," Kara said, choking up a little. The bathroom was sparkling clean. There were lavender curtains on either side of the one window. Most of all, she liked the double skylight above, showing off the colorful floor tiles below. There was a fully enclosed glass shower, large enough for two people. She saw two rain shower heads in it, as well.

"This is not a man's bathroom. This reminds me of someone who truly understands color and design."

"That's Mom's influence," he said with a chuckle. Walking to the linen closet, he opened it and laid out a fuchsia bath towel, hand towel, and wash cloth, setting them on the double sink counter. "These are yours." He pulled open another drawer and said, "Mom has a thing for Herbaria soap," and he pointed to ten different types of handmade soap. "Come and pick out your favorite organically made soap."

Moving opposite him, looking into the drawer, she smiled. "Oh, I love handmade soap!" and she reached out, trailing her fingers over the wrapped bars. "Citrus oatmeal," she murmured, curious and picking it up, holding to her nose. "Mmmm, this is like inhaling the fragrance of orange blossoms, Cade. I'll take this one."

His smile broadened. "It's my mom's favorite fragrance, too. Looks like you two have the same taste."

Placing the bar on top of her towels, she said, "I've met her quite often in Clayton. I just never realized how talented she really is. I'd love to see her watercolors. She never told me she painted. I wish she had."

Cade roused himself and pushed away from the door jamb, pulling his hands out of his pockets. "She's shy about her art. Come into my office. There's a computer in there, as well as Wi-Fi for the entire house. You can use the office any time you want."

Kara followed him down the hall. Each room was different from the other, featuring another pastel wall color. The floors were either pecan wood or a pastel-colored tile with throw rugs or area carpet. Cade opened a door and gestured her to go on in. She stepped inside and he followed. There was a heavy double oak desk, obviously an antique, and two ergonomic, modern chairs on either side of it. The walls were cream colored with pecan wood floors. This room had a more masculine presence. She could see a lot of wooden oak file cabinets and other office furniture sitting across from the huge desk.

"Mom calls this my 'Texas 1850s' room," he deadpanned, a smile lurking at the corners of his mouth. "I've always liked antiques and found this oak desk at a Goodwill store in McAllen. I found the English banquet oil lamp with the hand-painted flowers with the amethyst colored font around it at another Goodwill store in Houston. The frosted tulip shade is decorated with daisies. I kept the kerosene glass lamp that sits in the middle of it, but changed it from an oil lamp to an electric one."

"I love antiques," Kara sighed. "And this looks like a room straight out of Texas in the 1850s."

"Note the pecan wood floor too," he said proudly.

"It's beautiful."

"There was an old wooden floor that was going to be destroyed in an old home near McAllen. I drove down there one weekend and pulled up all the wood and brought it home and laid it in here. Paid the guys who were going to renovate it a hundred bucks. Everyone won in that exchange. That's how this room got its name."

"I can tell it's really old because it has that marvelous golden sheen that pecan wood always gets when it ages."

"It went well with the oak desk I already had," he said. "You can come in here and use my computer, or if you want to use your laptop, just set it up and I'll give you my password to hook into my network."

"Thanks, I probably will." She turned, looking at a four-by-five-foot framed watercolor painting hanging on the wall above where the desk sat. "Is this your mom's work?" she asked, lightly touching the oak frame around it.

Cade walked over and stood in front of the desk. "Yes, it is. Mom paints a lot of Texas subjects, like this rancher on a horse driving his cattle. Dad had taken us over to the King Ranch, which is in the area, and Mom brought her camera. She was thrilled with the trip. The one shot was cowboys on horseback driving a small herd of Santa Gertrudis cattle across a pasture."

Studying it, Kara said, "Your mother could be a professional. This is beautiful, Cade." Lifting her chin, she absorbed his nearness, just a few scant feet separated them. "Does she sell her art?"

"Nah, she doesn't think it's good enough to see the light of day. I've pleaded with her for years to send jpegs of her work to Houston and Dallas art galleries, but she won't do it. I think she's afraid of rejection, so she doesn't get her work out to the public to appreciate."

Giving him a wicked look, Kara said, "Like mother, like son, huh? It's okay to be humble about your work, Cade, but you shouldn't hide your talents under a bushel basket. Did you know someone would pay thousands of dollars for your mom's painting? She's no amateur."

"Well," he sighed, wrapping his arms across his chest, "I've tried to tell her that. When Dad suddenly died of a heart attack, we had no income any more. Mom is a high school graduate and was always a housewife before that happened. She married my dad when they were eighteen. When he passed away, she got a job at the local McDonald's and that's how she kept our heads above the financial waters as I grew up. I took odd jobs around the town, mowing grass and such, and between us, we survived. She worked sometimes twelve to sixteen hours a day, trying to get enough money to pay our monthly bills and the mortgage on our house."

"But I was told your mom had to declare bankruptcy and you *did* lose your home. Did that happen?" Kara saw the momentary pain of that memory in his eyes.

"Yes, she did but we survived that too. And the whole time she kept painting and refining her techniques throughout my growing up years. When I left for the Marine Corps after graduating from high school, I started sending half of my paycheck home to her so she could quit working at McDonald's. She didn't want to quit because the employees are like family to one another, but she did cut down her hours, allowing herself more free time to paint."

"You've been a wonderful son to her," Kara said quietly, reaching out, resting her hand on his arm, feeling his biceps beneath the fabric of his khaki shirt respond to her touch. She wanted to trail her fingers down his lean, muscular arm and explore him. There was a change in his eyes as well, more golden tones in their depths.

She felt his muscles tighten momentarily beneath her fingers. Kara's heart thudded once to underscore the sudden sexual tension swirling between them. Her thighs tightened, wanting him to explore her. What was happening between them? Whatever it was, it was clearly mutual and that alone stunned Kara.

For the first time, she saw hunger and desire in Cade's eyes as he held her upturned gaze. All those years as a child and later, as a teen growing up with him as a quiet shadow in her life, they had never really met, never really talked. And yet, her mind spun back to those twelve years they'd shared, an economic chasm stood between them at the time. But her heart, oh her heart had *always* been drawn to humble, silent Cade Patterson. When she saw him on the football field, he was her hero. How many dreams had she spun around him? Too many to count.

And right now he was standing inches away from her. She inhaled his masculine scent, saw the fire burning deep in his eyes that he held for her alone. Every inch of her body responded to that heated look. Cade Patterson had just stepped out of the shadows of her life and into the light of day. He was letting her know in no uncertain terms that he desired her. The revelation blind-sided her.

But it was in the best of ways because Kara had secrets of her own she carried about him in her heart. She wondered if Cade realized just how much she had yearned for him over the years. None of it had ever been given voice in any form.

Searching his gaze, her fingertips tightened around his hard, muscled arm. The change in his eyes was instantaneous, narrowing, as if she was his quarry and he was going to capture her. A frisson of desire erupted in her lower body, flashing to life, flowing upward, tightening her nipples, her mind melting beneath his intense look—one that spoke directly to her lonely heart. This meeting had been a long time coming. But now, it was here.

CHAPTER 5

WHERE HAD THE last two weeks gone? Kara had just towel dried herself off after taking a long, hot soak in the garden tub in Cade's home. Her heart beat with happiness. She placed the bright yellow towel on the rack, smoothing it out. She'd just gotten home from Delos and Cade was out in the kitchen, fixing them a dinner of chili and homemade jalapeño cornbread he'd whipped up.

Glancing in the mirror with steam curling around the edges, she touched her left cheek. Her black eye was gone and the swelling on her cheek finally looked normal once more. Although she was sure she looked like a troll to Cade, he never mentioned how distorted looking her face was for those weeks. Her nose looked as if it had never been broken, much to her relief.

But law enforcement had not found Fuentes, the man who had assaulted her, and that bothered her more than anything else. She was now finding herself afraid of her own shadow, except when she was in Cade's home. Here, she felt safe—and desirable.

Yet, Cade remained the perfect gentleman, never flirting with her, never touching her, or making a move to let her know he wanted her. Kara had seen the desire in his eyes from time to time but he never acted on it.

She climbed into a pair of comfy white linen pants and a pink tee with cap sleeves. Kara quickly ran a comb through her hair, smoothing it into place. One thing she'd noticed was that Cade enjoyed seeing her with her hair down. Sometimes when they were watching a TV show, she would glance up and he'd be studying her with a tender look that gripped her heart and made her momentarily breathless. It was as if her father's edict that he was from the wrong side of the tracks and had to keep his hands off her still sat silently between them, a moat that could never be crossed.

She hated that. More and more, Kara was reaching out to Cade to let him know she *invited* his touch, his attention, and that she liked it. Now, she would lie awake for an hour or more at night in the huge bed alone, trying to think of subtle, nonverbal ways to let Cade know she was interested in him personally, woman-to-man.

So what was stopping him? Frustration swirled and eddied through her as she pulled her fingers through her straight sable hair, watching the darker strands along with the gold highlighted ones, tangle through the sable color. She saw interest in Cade's eyes when she'd catch him staring at her. It wasn't that he did it often. He didn't. Just—sometimes, her heart would catch, beat a little harder and her whole body went on alert, an ache building deep within her for him alone.

Did her father's harsh warning to him when he was a young boy keep him in a strangle hold? Did he still see her as unapproachable? Untouchable? Her lips thinned as she slipped her feet into a pair of white sandals.

Maybe it would take a confrontation with Cade, telling him how her feelings were growing for him, that she was deeply interested in him, and wanted to explore what they might have together. Wasn't it obvious to him by now that she was her own woman? Her father no longer ran and controlled her life. She made her own decisions.

More frustration rose within her. Sometimes men could be so thick-headed! It seemed to be a disease they all had. Setting the comb aside, she cleaned up in the bathroom, opened the door, and walked out into her beautiful bedroom.

Kara never tired of looking at Cade's mosaic wildflower panel above the bed. She had a dream last night that they were making love in this bed and she looked up to see the beauty and color of the flowers. The dream had stayed with her all day at the school and her lower body felt achy and needy this evening.

Living with Cade was turning her into a hormonal wreck. She wanted him so badly that it was all she'd thought about the past week.

Putting her dirty clothes in a nearby hamper, she inhaled the spicy scent of chili wafting through the partly open bedroom door. Cade liked quiet music in the background. Most of it was bluegrass or country music, but what Texan didn't like those kinds of songs and instrumentals? She smiled, pushing her palms down the sides of her linen pants, hurrying out of the room and down the hall.

They'd fallen into a rhythm with one another at dinner time. She made the salad and set the table. He did all the serious cooking. She'd been right about Cade being a gourmet chef—that Wolf stove was more than just a showpiece. He loved to cook and she often thought that his mosaic works were just another extension of his artistic nature.

Cade loved creating things and combining them, like a mad scientist, curious about how things fit together. He used colorful pieces of broken ceramic tiles and pieced them together to create beautiful mosaic pictures. His use of spices enhanced the food he was cooking and was another art form. He used those same skills in his police work as a deputy sheriff investigating a crime scene for puzzle-like clues.

The August sunlight was bright, filling the open-concept room that included the kitchen with bright, rich color. Kara was grateful for the air conditioning, knowing how hot and humid the Texas Gulf Coast could become.

She watched as Cade stood at the stove and a new tenderness swept through her. His mother, Tracy, had actually sewn him what she called "manly aprons," mostly khaki and without fanciness or frills. He'd come home and shed his deputy sheriff's gear and put on an old, worn pair of Levis, his beat-up boots and a long-sleeved white cowboy shirt. He certainly looked sexy with the sleeves rolled up and cuffed to just below his elbows. And he was even sexier in that manly apron. Cade was so confident about who he was, in his masculinity, that he could wear an apron without apology. She approached from the side, knowing he didn't like her to quietly move up behind him for good reason. She saw the veins standing out along his lower arms as he slowly stirred a large pot of chili with a long wooden spoon.

"Smells good," she said, halting near the end of the stove, absorbing his intent profile. There were several jars of spices sitting nearby and she was sure he was working on getting the chili to taste just right. His mouth drew upward and he twisted a look in her direction.

"Hope you're hungry, Ms. Knight."

"Starving. Ever since you let me stay here, I must have gained five pounds and its all your fault, Patterson." She loved when he laughed, as he did just then. It was a rolling rumble within that exquisitely broad, deep chest of his.

"That extra weight looks good on you," he teased, taking one last taste of his chili. "You were underweight when you came here, Kara."

She leaned her hip against the counter, enjoying watching him as he tasted his spiced chili. A look of pleasure wreathed his face and he licked his lips. "Want a test taste?" He scooped up a bit of the juice from the top of the twelve-quart stainless steel pot and into the wooden spoon. He blew on it to cool it for her.

"Sure," she said, coming close, her breast brushing lightly against his upper arm. He held one hand beneath the spoon and guided it toward her opening lips. Her eyes never left his as she tasted the warm juice. There was such hunger in his eyes and it sure wasn't for food. It was for her.

"Mmmm," she said, moving away enough so that she no longer had contact with his body, "That is so good, Cade." She watched him hesitate, as if torn about something. He nodded and set the spoon aside.

"I like pleasing you, Kara," he said gruffly, holding her gaze, unmoving.

There was such a powerful energy that suddenly sprang up between them that Kara felt faint. Cade was going to kiss her. She saw it in his golden eyes, saw the intent. Only inches separated them. Her whole body swayed forward as he slowly lifted his hands toward her face. His palms were rough, his fingers calloused and strong. He held his passion back as much as he could as he cupped her chin.

Tilting it up just a fraction, she stared deeply into his narrowing eyes, her breath hitching, her heart suddenly taking off at a gallop. This had been coming and never had Kara wanted a man to kiss her more than Cade Patterson. Did he know how long she'd ached as a blossoming teenager to kiss those sculpted lips of his? To taste him? To feel his power unleashed and shared with her?

Leaning down, he brushed his lips against her brow. "Kara, I want to kiss you…but it has to be mutual…"

Cade's low, growling tone feathered through her. He caressed her cheeks with his thumbs. She could feel the callouses from the work he did at a nearby ranch, herding cattle, doing wrangling chores, whenever he could get a day off. For him it was extra money, and she'd come to discover he was an earnest saver for the future. It was a good habit to have and she admired his ability to work hard and be responsible. She loved that about him.

Would Cade think her a romantic if she told him she saw the sun, the moon, and all the stars in the sky in his intense golden eyes that now held hers? She stepped forward, pressing her body against the front of his in response to his question. Without a word, she raised up on her toes, meeting his descending mouth. There was such sweetness flowing through her as his lips settled against hers, tentative, seeing if she wanted his contact. A low sound vibrated in the back of Kara's throat and his fingers tightened slightly, holding her against him as he invited her to return the gift of himself to her.

All Kara was aware of in that moment was his restrained power as a man, holding himself in tight check as she parted her lips, opening up to him, telling him in a silent language of her own need for him. Her hands flattened against his chest, the soft cotton material of his shirt revealing the male warmth of his flesh beneath her palms. His mouth drew her more deeply into his, gliding across her lips, molding hers to his, drinking in the sensation of her lips as if she were an exquisite wine Cade had tasted for the first time. So many sensations overwhelmed Kara in that moment. She was transported, unable to think, only able to feel.

He released her face, his hands trailing down either side of her slender neck, flowing across her shoulders, pulling her toward his hard, lean body to create full contact between them. It was such a sensual movement that she felt dampness between her thighs. Never had a man turned her on so swiftly! His breath was moist against her cheek, his scent a combination of the sage soap he used and the scent of chili, the heat of the spices combining to pull a sound of pleasure from deep within her.

Time melted around Kara. Her whole world anchored to each ragged breath of his that flowed into her own. Cade's mouth grew more firm and confident as he coaxed her to meet him all the way. It was mutual. She was no wilting lily when it came to engaging and moving with her own female needs. As his palm skated slowly down her spine toward her hips, it felt as if Cade were memorizing her in every possible way. Fire skittered downward through her as he took her mouth, unleashing some of his tightly held strength, sharing himself more fully with her. The moment his large, exploring hands settled around her hips, she felt him place himself in check.

His mouth slowly separated from hers. He kissed each of her closed eyelids and reluctantly eased Kara slightly away from him.

Opening her eyes, feeling sexual languor, her lower body aching with need, she stared, dazed, into his darkening eyes now filled with pure hunger.

"What...," she whispered. His hands smoothed her hips, stroking her, calming her. She wanted to make love with this man.

"This has been a long time coming," Cade rasped, his gaze locked with hers. Lifting one hand, he moved a few strands of her sable hair away from her one cheek. "I wasn't sure of what we have, Kara...we have a past. A long one."

Her brows dipped and she so badly wanted to lean into him, feel his body against hers once more, but he held her so she couldn't connect fully with him. It was then she realized that Cade was as confused as she was. He was trying to put his feelings into words, but her mind wasn't working at all. Her sensual side had exploded and taken over everything, including her ability to think.

"So what?" she managed, her voice strained. Again, she saw hesitation come to his expression as he searched her widening eyes. "The past is the past, Cade. I don't care about it. We can't change it, anyway. Let it go." She was beginning to sound strident and upset. And she was.

"It's not easy to let the past not affect the present," he offered, sliding his hand across her hair, taming it back into place here and there. "We still live in Kenedy County. Your father doesn't approve of me and never will. For him, time stands still. He doesn't care who I am, what I've become, or what I do for a living. I'll always be from the wrong side of the tracks with him, Kara."

"I'm not my father!" she cried, her fingers curling against his chest. "I've *never* been like him! I don't believe for one second you or anyone in Clayton is beneath me! He's controlling, Cade.

He belittles people, intimidates them. But I'm an adult and so are you. We don't need to worry about that now."

Giving her a patient look, Cade asked, "What if I loved you right now, Kara? What if we decided to extend our relationship, live with one another? Maybe dream even bigger dreams together? What would your father do then, I wonder?" He gave her a keen look, leaning down, kissing her forehead.

"I left my father's ranch at eighteen, Cade and never returned! I refused to be a pawn of his any more. I turned down the job he offered me. I'm my own woman now, not his imprisoned child that he can manipulate like before." Her voice became choked. "Please, you have to believe me," she said giving him a pleading look. The glint in his eyes changed and she saw pain deep in them, the fact that her father had demeaned his entire family for eighteen years.

Kara understood Cade's hurt, their collective past staining their present. Why hadn't she realized that kissing Cade would bring up all of these issues to discuss? It had to happen she realized belatedly. They had so much to talk about, to sort out before they could go any farther with one another. If only she could tell Cade how many times she'd dreamed of having a relationship with him.

"I do believe you, Kara. But we have to talk. You have to grasp that once your father realizes there is something serious between us, he may well lash out at you, or me, or both of us. We've both seen what he did to boys in high school who chased you and wanted a relationship with you." His mouth thinned. "I don't want that to happen now. I realize we're adults and we're old enough to decide what's best for ourselves. But Jud Knight has never realized that and I don't believe he ever will. When I came home from the Corps, I found out you were still single. I asked my mother if you were with anyone and she said no, that your father had chased off a guy who had serious intentions toward you. He ended up in an accident that nearly took his life from what I understand."

All her hopes for Cade being a part of her life felt like a balloon deflating right in front of her. Kara wearily rested her brow against his chest, feeling hot tears stinging the insides of her lids. Just the slow sweep of his hand against her back brought back her hope.

"That's true," she said in a low, strained tone. "Bill Curdy was serious about me and yes, we had a relationship. He lived in Houston. But what we had was a friendship, not the serious relationship my father thought it was. Bill was a nice guy but he was a truck driver, Cade. There was an accident north of Houston and he nearly died in that crash." She felt his hands warm with promise on her shoulders, felt him press a kiss to her hair.

"What was the cause of the accident?" he

demanded.

"Someone cut the brake fluid line. The police said it had been done on purpose, but they never found out who did it."

"Was your father behind it?"

Lifting her head, her eyes swimming with tears, she whispered brokenly, "I think so. I can't prove it, though. My father hires men to go after anyone who shows any interest toward me. After Bill nearly died, I swore off being seen with men, Cade. That is…until you walked back into my life," she said, sobbing. She pressed her hand against her lips and stared at him. Was her father capable of murder? In her heart, Kara knew the answer. He was. Every man who had shown interest in her had had an accident of some sort. A vehicle would run the guy off the road, the brake fluid line would get cut, someone would fire a gun into the driver's side window, barely missing the driver. It was too much. Just too much.

BRINGING HER AGAINST him, Cade held Kara, resting his chin against her head. He could feel her trembling, her fingers digging convulsively into his shirt, the fabric becoming wet with her silently spilled tears. She was trying so hard to stop from crying. He could feel her struggle and he kissed her temple, his lips near her ear. "Kara, you're carrying around too much by yourself. I'll hold you…let it go."

And she did. A sob tore out of her, shaking her entire body. The sounds coming out of her were as if she were an animal in horrific pain. Cade knew Jud Knight despised anyone who cried, even a woman. He knew enough in the time that Kara had lived with him that her father was a tyrant of unbelievable proportions. As gentle and kind as his own father had been to him and his mother, Jud Knight was the opposite—a monster inside a man's body as far as he was concerned. As he held Kara in his embrace, rocking her a little, trying to soothe her, Cade made her a silent promise. He loved Kara. He had always loved her from the first time he'd seen her in the first grade, and that love had only grown through the years as they went through school together. She didn't know it, but that didn't matter. Cade would surround her with his protection because he loved her. And this time, her father wasn't going to interfere with what was blossoming naturally between them now.

No, Jud Knight wasn't going to chase him off. Not ever again.

As he slid his hand slowly up and down her back, he felt Kara's weeping begin to slowly abate. A woman crying tore him up, but not in the same way it did Jud. Cade felt helpless and wanted to fix whatever was wrong so Kara wouldn't want to cry any more. She was in such pain.

She was all heart and she'd always worn her emotions on her sleeve. All she'd ever wanted out of her life was to improve the lives of other people who had less than she did.

He knew now that Kara was his whole world and unless she objected to it, Cade would surround her not only with his love, but his protection.

Leaning toward the counter, he grabbed the box of tissues and pulled a few free, stuffing them gently into her damp hand. Her fingers trembled as she tried to stop the trickle of tears, her eyes reddened by the release. But it was a good release and Cade knew it, continuing to soothe her with his light but caring touch.

"Come on," he urged her quietly, releasing her and tucking her beneath his arm and against his body, "Let's go sit down in the living room."

"B-but the chili," Kara brokenly protested, twisting her head, looking toward the stove.

"I shut it off earlier. It will sit there and be fine. We can eat later when we feel like it." Cade guided her to the couch that she loved sitting on, her knees drawn up to her chest, reading a book or knitting. Her mother had taught her how to knit when she was ten-years-old. Kara admitted it calmed her anxiety that seemed to come and go every day.

Cade had watched her covertly during the time she'd spent with him. He'd found that her sleep was often restless and broken, that anxiety would wake her up. When she was anxious, she chewed on her nearly non-existent fingernails and she'd always pull out her knitting bag and work on some project. She'd confided that she made sweaters for all the children who came to the Delos Home School and Day Care Center. She would make them throughout the summer and then wrap each one in a pretty Christmas box with a shiny red or green ribbon. Each child received a gift from her, no matter his or her age.

It was just another aspect of Kara that Cade loved. She was a giver, not a taker. Her father however, was a brutal taker. He sucked the life out of everything he owned or touched. He was sure her father was also brutal to his wife, Pamela, who was known around the county as a kind, generous woman. How was she able to live with that kind of person?

Sitting down in the corner of the sofa, Cade coaxed Kara into his arms. She came, lifting her legs and tucking them beneath her, her head coming to rest on his shoulder, hand against his chest. She was pale, her beautiful eyes reddened and filled with anguish. He eased the curtain of long, sable hair away from her face so he could watch her expressions as they talked. This was what they both needed: intimacy and nurturing. He could feel her trusting him with her life, the anxiety dissolving in her expression the longer he held her.

Closing her eyes, Kara rested her cheek against him, whispering hoarsely, "Do you know how long I've wished you would hold me just like this, Cade?"

He shook his head, his hand coming to rest over her hair. "No, I had no idea."

"Forever," she whispered. "Forever."

"That's a long time, Kara."

Lifting her chin, she stared up at him. "I remember seeing you in the first grade and thinking you were so cute, so nice. I was drawn to you even then, Cade. I remember going home that first day and telling my parents that I liked you so much." Her voice filled with hurt. "My father got angry. He said you were the son of a plumber and you were beneath us. You were poor. You would never amount to anything. He ordered me to never talk to you again, to stay away from you, or he'd hurt you."

Cade stilled. "He said that?" He was stunned by her revelation.

"I was only six-years-old. My mother yelled at my father for yelling at me like that. I sat at the table, starting to cry. It was a horrible end to a wonderful day." She dabbed her eyes with the damp tissue. "I remember my mom talking to me in my room. She was telling me not to talk to you or be found walking around with you, or Father might hurt you. I couldn't understand it at that age, Cade. But I believed my mother. From then on, I had to like you from afar. I was so afraid my father would harm you. I'd seen him hit some of the wranglers who worked for us. I was always afraid that someday he'd hit me or my mom."

Cade said nothing for a moment as rage flooded through him. "He began to threaten you when you were that young?"

Kara bobbed her head, saying nothing, just burrowing her face into his chest, as if to hide. He eased his other arm around her and just held her. Finally, after a few minutes, the tension left her body and he heard her draw in a ragged sigh and then release it.

"Well," he began, "since we're fessing up to one another, I remember seeing you in our classroom in first grade. I thought you were a fairytale princess dropped into the room. That was how pretty you looked to me and I was only six at the time."

"I-I didn't know. We couldn't have known what the other thought. I had to avoid you, Cade, or I knew my father would make good on his promise."

"The man is an animal." Cade's anger was reaching the breaking point and he couldn't keep it out of his voice.

"You think? After I got out of there at eighteen, I took teaching classes at Texas A&M. I also had to take a number of psychology classes." She wiped her nose. "That was when I realized my father was sociopathic. He had no feelings, no morals, no values. He played by his own rules."

"And that's why, when you returned to Clayton to set up that Delos school, you refused to live on his ranch?"

"Exactly. I was going to be my own person. My mother supported me, even though my father used to scream and curse at her for standing up for me and my decisions."

"Why hasn't your mother left him?" Cade demanded, voicing a question he'd asked himself often since reconnecting with Kara.

Wearily, she replied, "I don't know. I wish I did. I don't understand it. She's often told me he's like a mad, sick dog and someone has to take care of him. She always had a soft spot in her heart for strays. That's why she works for the county humane society and gives money to no-kill shelters."

"God," he muttered, shaking his head. "What the hell happened to him to make him like this, Kara?"

"I was having lunch with my mom at Clayton Cafe once and asked her that shortly after I graduated from the university. She said his father, Gordon Knight, my grandfather, used a belt on him. Any time he did something wrong, he got taken to the barn and whipped. My father turned into an angry, vengeful teenager and he managed to get his court records sealed."

"Oh?" Cade asked, pulling her away from him to meet her red, swollen eyes. "Was he arrested as a teen here in Kenedy County?"

"Yes." Kara sat up, sweeping her hair off her face, scrubbing her cheeks dry of the last remaining tears. "Mom said he committed arson at thirteen and burned down a man's barn at a nearby ranch because he didn't like him. That fire killed thirty of the man's prized horses, Cade. It was awful."

Her voice shook with grief. "He spent time in juvenile hall but because of his rich, powerful father, he got out in a few months. The court records were sealed, never to see the light of day again."

"Anything else?" Cade's mind spun with possibilities. It would take a lot to get Knight's court records unsealed and he'd have to have a damn good reason to make that request in the first place to see what was contained in them.

"My father worked with a Mexican drug cartel until he was eighteen. They ran drugs from the border near McCall. It's not something I'm proud of, believe me. I've never touched drugs and never will. I see what it does to the person and how it hurts the whole family."

"What happened when Jud was eighteen?"

"My grandfather made him foreman of the ranch, took him under his wing, and taught him how to run and manage the ranch. I guess at that time, my father was old enough, thoroughly brainwashed and controlled enough by my grandfather that he no longer got beaten up like he used to."

Moving his thumb across her damp, pale cheek, Cade looked into her pain-filled eyes. "Did your father ever lay a hand on you?"

"No," Kara pressed her cheek against his opened palm, closing her eyes for a moment, needing his continued touch because he comforted her. "Just verbal and emotional abuse."

She was minimizing it with a shrug of her shoulders, but Cade also knew a lot about psychology because he too had taken courses for his law enforcement degree. "It doesn't matter whether it's verbal, emotional, mental, or physical abuse, Kara. The body is under attack and the person is threatened, regardless."

"Yes, I know," she murmured, lying her head against his chest, content to remain just the way she was.

When a person was under threat, it automatically brought up a lot of anxiety, as Cade knew too well. Family abuse equated directly with PTSD in combat ground troops. Only this time, the war was within Kara's family and went on every day for the first eighteen years of her life. Now, it painted a far clearer picture for him about her moments of high anxiety, which seemed to strike out of nowhere almost daily. He'd seen that she got anxious around nine p.m. and there had been mornings when he'd awakened and heard her out in the kitchen at five a.m. He'd get up and come out to see if she was all right.

She told him she was anxious and was getting up for a glass of water. Then, she would return to bed. Cade didn't try and talk to her at those times, sensing something was terribly wrong because he could see the terror banked in her drowsy eyes.

Smoothing his hand over her back, removing a few wrinkles across her tee, he asked, "Do you have any memory of something traumatic happening to you at nine p.m.?"

"Oh," she mumbled, rubbing her cheek against his chest, nuzzling deeper into his arms, "that…"

"What's 'that'?"

"When I was seven, drug runners from Mexico broke into our ranch property. They drove four pickups around and around the main house. I had been asleep at the time, but bullets came flying through the window next to my bed. I woke up terrorized. My mother ran into my bedroom, shrieking my name, dragging me off the bed, covering me with her body while we huddled on the floor. More bullets came through the bedroom wall after that."

Scowling, Cade said, "Was this a rival drug gang that your father had fought against when he was running drugs?"

"You can go search the sheriff's database on that one," Kara murmured, slipping her hand up across his chest, moving her fingers across his shoulder. "There was an investigation and they found it was another drug cartel trying to horn into the Gomez cartel's area. They had a big fight with them and drove them out."

"But why would they attack your ranch, Kara? That doesn't make sense. Was your father still running drugs for the Gomez cartel? Hiding them somewhere on his ranch?"

"I don't know, Cade. I was only seven at the time. I was terrified, I couldn't stop crying and shaking. My mother was just as traumatized by the attack as I was."

"Did it ever happen before or since that time?"

"No."

"Tell me about five a.m. You keep waking up at that time and you always look scared to me, Kara. Do you have any memory of that time?"

"I was ten," she began, her voice low and off key. "My father has three huge barns. They're all three stories high. For as long as I could remember I was told *never* to go into barn number three. I woke up one time, it was winter, and the clock read five a.m. I heard the sounds of big trucks and I couldn't understand what was going on or why they were at our ranch so early. I pulled on my winter coat, my socks and boots, and hurried out the back door. I saw a huge truck with Mexico license plates backing up to barn number three. It was a clear morning, cold, and I saw my father and three wranglers off to one side, giving hand signals to the truck. There was another semi-truck nearby, a normal type that you see on any interstate in the U.S. It had no markings on it, but both its doors were open."

"What happened next?"

"I could hear my father cursing and yelling at our ranch hands. I hid in some shrubs near the corner of our house. There was light coming from outside the barn and I could see the men and trucks. As soon as the truck with the Mexico plates stopped, two men ran over to it and opened the doors." She swallowed hard, forcing the words from between her lips. "There were men, women, and children being herded like cattle toward the other truck. They slapped, yelled, and shoved them toward it. Someone had put a plank of wood up so they could scramble up into it."

Frowning, Cade asked, "Illegal trafficking?"

"I think so. At the time, I didn't understand who they were or what they were doing here on our ranch. I was very confused and scared that I'd be seen by my father. There must have been fifty people herded off in that one truck. The kids were crying. Some of the women screamed and tried to run away, but the wranglers caught them and pushed them back into line to get into the truck."

He felt her tensing, as if she were trying to protect herself because a blow was coming her way. Gently, Cade moved his hand across her shoulders. "It's all right. Tell me what you can."

"One woman lost her little boy's hand. He must have been all of six. He ran because he was so scared. One of the wranglers went after him and jerked him by the arm and he went flying through the air. When he landed, he screamed. I think he broke his arm when he hit the ground."

Tightening his embrace around her, Cade cursed softly. He felt her burrowing as deep as she could into his arms, seeking protection. "I'm sorry," he said thickly, kissing her temple, wanting to take away her pain, that memory that haunted her to this day. "What happened then?"

"I didn't remember the rest of what I saw for years afterward, Cade." She pulled away, studying his tight features, the flash of anger in his eyes. "I was thirteen when it all came rushing back to me. Before that I would have nightmares of that night. Every time I saw that poor child landing in the dirt, I'd scream. It was always around five a.m. when I awoke from that nightmare."

Cade whispered her name, kissing her brow and cheek. "I'm so damned sorry you had to see that, Kara. Kids are easily traumatized. I wish…I wish I could remove it from your memory but I know that's not going to happen."

"Even worse, Cade, I never got up the guts to confront my father and ask him about that night after the memory returned. I was too scared of him. He had stood there and let one of his wranglers harm that child. What kind of monster is he?" she said, searching his angry gaze.

"No wonder you wanted the hell out of there when you turned eighteen."

Grimly, she said, "Yes and I'm never going back. It was a prison, Cade, the worst kind. At least," she said, gesturing with her hand, "I'm free now. I'm doing something I love. I'm making a difference or at least I'm trying to."

"You do," he reassured her, sliding his hand to her cheek, drawing her against his chest. "And you'll continue to because that's who you are."

"That's why I'm so afraid of what happened to me, Cade. I wonder if this guy who assaulted me is with another drug cartel," she said, searching his eyes.

"I don't know, but we have to find out." Then, changing the subject he said, "You're probably not hungry right now."

She shook her head and began gnawing on that sad thumbnail, "You probably are, though."

"Let's just sit here for awhile longer. You need to come down off that cliff you're on."

"Oh, my anxiety…"

"Yeah. Just settle in, close your eyes and rest. You're safe here, Kara. I'll protect you. You can count on it."

CHAPTER 6

KARA FELL ASLEEP almost immediately. Cade understood that she was exhausted from the emotional deluge, all those years of carrying those childhood memories around inside her, coupled with the assault. No wonder, she was totaled.

He carried her to his bed and covered her up with a soft pink afghan that she'd brought with her from her house. Even in sleep, she curled into what he called a "fetal position" on her right side, knees drawn up tight against her body. He was sure that it started when she was a very young child, living in that threatening environment created by her father.

He stood there, wavering. Wanting her. Wanting to love her until she forgot all the injuries to her soul. But it wouldn't have been right. He would be taking advantage of her trust in him. If Kara had wanted sex, she'd have initiated it with him. Cade knew her well enough by now to know she wasn't shy about showing her affection to him. *The little vixen.* Turning, he left the bedroom door slightly ajar so some light from the hallway could drive away the total darkness within the room.

Walking quietly, he went to the kitchen and got a bowl of chili, adding some shredded sharp cheddar cheese and a dollop of sour cream on top. As he ate at the table, the quiet bluegrass music playing in the background, Cade replayed Kara's conversation with him. As a deputy, he'd seen frightened children and adults in trauma and shock. It impacted him greatly because he'd always been affected by human suffering, especially with children. Until now, he'd never heard a word uttered about Jud Knight at the sheriff's headquarters.

His commander, Tom Atkinson, was in his early sixties, lean as a rail post, with thirty years of law enforcement experience under his belt. He'd been born in Clayton and grown up in this county. Cade would bet a month's worth of pay that Atkinson, burned dark by the Texas sun over the decades, would know a helluva lot more about Knight and his illegal activities. Or did he? His boss wasn't the type to turn his head the other way regarding any law breaker. Grimly, Cade reminded himself that he gave permission to allow Kara to remain at his home. That had surprised him because it seemed to Cade to go against law enforcement common sense.

Atkinson had said the only reason he was giving Kara a choice between his home and her father's ranch, was because of Jud's power in the county. At this point, Cade wondered if Jud Knight wasn't politically funding his boss's campaign because he was running for reelection. Cade knew after being on the job for only a year that he didn't discern all the political realities that ran the department. Spooning the hot, spicy chili into his mouth, he kept trying to ignore thoughts of Kara's soft kiss.

Cade couldn't imagine ten-year-old Kara seeing another child injured so brutally as on the night the illegal immigrants were herded into the semi-truck. Was her mother, Pamela, aware of the trucks coming in? Had she seen any of this happen? If she had and it wasn't reported...

The unanswered questions Cade had left him uneasy. This was a federal crime. He needed to talk with Kara more about this incident. As a ten-year-old child, she would not be expected to turn her father or the wrangler who injured that child, over to the U.S. Border Patrol. The Knight family was a completely dysfunctional family run by a madman as far as he was concerned. Cade had always been grateful he had two very loving parents who cherished him and did not abuse him. So often as a law enforcement officer, he saw the dark, lurid underbelly of human society. Fifty percent of the people he'd met as a deputy should never have been allowed to be parents.

They left their innocent youngsters at high risk, were irresponsible parents, and were either uncaring or abusive toward their children.

There were days like this that he didn't like being a deputy. He'd seen enough fighting in Afghanistan but family wars were another form of combat, the children always the losers. Scowling, he ate the last crumb of the jalapeño cornbread he'd baked earlier and finished off the last spoonful of chili from the bottom of his bowl. If Kara woke up later and was coherent, he'd like to ask her more about the trafficking that Jud Knight had been involved in. Was he still part of a trafficking ring? There was too much drug activity in this county to be sure of anything or anyone and Cade knew it. A careful investigation would have to be approved by Atkinson first and he was going to approach his boss about this incident. But would he be able trust his boss?

If only Kara would sleep through the night. She seemed to enjoy being here with him and was no longer as stressed out as before. He knew that the toll of shock took weeks, months, or sometimes years, depending upon the nature of the trauma, to leave a person. Kara was still in a major healing curve and terribly vulnerable, so he didn't want to take advantage of her in that state.

They were powerfully drawn to one another, no question, but her attacker was still on the loose. Had Fuentes faded back across the border and back into Mexico? Perhaps, but Cade wasn't willing to allow Kara to return her home and be there alone just yet and the Sheriff Atkinson was in agreement. Until they could absolutely verify it one way or another, Atkinson wanted Kara to remain at his home. Instead, over the past weeks, Cade had gone over to her home several times to clean it up.

Kara had wanted to do it but he'd dissuaded her. All it would do was increase her stress level once more, not lessen it. Whenever she could return home, she would find it tidy and clean, just as she'd left it that morning when she'd gone to work.

It was nearly nine p.m. when Cade heard a noise in the hall. He was sitting on the couch reading the county newspaper on his tablet and looked up. He saw Kara stumble sleepily down the hall, pushing her mussed hair off her face. He got up, seeing that she was barefoot and smiled, thinking she looked more like a ragamuffin in that moment, vulnerable and beautiful.

"Hi," she mumbled, aiming herself in his direction after she spotted him. "I'm thirsty."

Cade met her and she closed the distance, pressing her body against his, asking for his embrace as she nestled her brow against his jaw. Enclosing her with his arms, he murmured, "You're barefoot. I could step on your toes, Kara," he said, grinning a little, hearing a soft sound of protest come from her. He liked the way her arms tightened around his waist, liked it way too much, hungrily absorbing her soft, curved body as she sank against his hard frame.

"You won't," she murmured sleepily, nuzzling his neck, pressing a small kiss upon it.

Her lips were velvet and pliant. Cade hadn't expected this affection and it rocked him as little else could. Had their one kiss torn down that old barrier that had always stood between them? He eased her beneath his arm and positioned her against him. "Let's go to the refrigerator. I have some cold bottled water in there."

"Mmmm, sounds wonderful," and she entrusted herself fully to him, allowing him to guide her.

"Did you sleep well?" he asked, opening the fridge, drawing out a bottle.

"I don't even remember dropping off, but yes, I did." Kara moved from beneath his arm as he reached into the cabinet for a clean glass. Rubbing her face, she muttered, "I feel better, though. Like I off-loaded a lifetime's worth of stuff, maybe." Giving him a questioning look, she added, "Maybe it was the kiss we shared?"

Cade poured the water. "Maybe it was." He watched her place the glass to her lower lip, lift her chin, the graceful line of her neck revealed as she drank deeply. Her face mirrored peace, her delft-colored eyes soft, shining with happiness. He was happy too, his whole body lighter after her unexpected affection. Barely able to think, his own heart pounding with urgency for Kara, he tried to tamp down his needs and expectations from her. She was obviously defenseless after just waking up, not quite here and not quite there. Even her tousled hair made her look excruciatingly wanton to Cade.

"Thanks," she whispered, setting the glass on the counter.

"Are you hungry?" he asked, peering into her barely opened eyes. Cade had discovered that Kara did not wake up easily. It was a process that involved at least two to three cups of coffee before she was alert.

Shrugging, she pushed away from the counter and came back to him, resting against his body, closing her eyes, her head against his chest as he placed his arms lightly around her shoulders. "I'm hungry, Cade, but maybe not for food…"

He caught the drift, his mouth lifting slightly. He celebrated her directness because people like that were easy to understand. What you saw, you got. No games. No masks. No manipulation. When Kara lifted her chin from his chest, searching his eyes, he felt like a five-alarm siren had gone off deep in his lower body. There was no disguising her lust and sexual interest.

"I kissed you earlier," she said. "I liked it, Cade. If you knew how long I've wanted to kiss you, I don't think you would believe me."

"Try me," he teased, rocking her hips against his. Fire flamed to life and Cade knew without a doubt that Kara was aware of his growing erection. There was no way to hide it because it felt as if they were welded hotly to one another's hips.

"First grade." Her brows moved upward and she laughed. "See? I told you that you wouldn't believe me! But it's the truth!"

"Hmmm, well, I have a confession to make too, Ms. Knight. You were magical to me. You always have been." He saw her expression grow pleased, the twinkle in her eyes making his heart long desperately for her.

"Well, Deputy Patterson? I'd say that the kiss we shared between us earlier is something we should both explore more. Don't you?"

The moment she moved her hips against his, he groaned. Heat poured through him, awakening him on every level. "I like a bold woman who knows what she wants."

"There are no wimpy women in Texas. You know that, Cade."

He chuckled. "There is this thing about a Texas woman," he agreed, leaning over, nuzzling her temple and inhaled her sweet scent. Cade waited to see how Kara would respond. Did she only want another kiss? Because the signals she was sending included a lot more than just a kiss and he didn't want to assume one damn thing with her.

"Mmmm, I love when you kiss me, Cade. You make every dream I ever had about you come true."

Easing her away from him so he could look into her slumberous, lust-filled eyes, he asked, "Tell me what you want, Kara."

"You."

He smiled a little. "I've always been yours, but from a distance before this. Are you sure about this? About us?"

"Never more sure than right now."

"Maybe this is because of what we talked about earlier that brought you to tears?"

Stubbornly, she shook her head, the waves of sable hair sliding across her shoulders. "No." And then, her jaw became firm, her eyes narrowing on him. "I want you, Cade. All of you. If you'll have me."

He understood the kind of courage it took for Kara to admit that. "I wanted to be your friend in the first grade, Kara." He saw relief come to her eyes, and then happiness shine in them. His heart exploded with incredible joy. Never, in a million years, had he thought this moment would ever happen. Even in his dreams, he'd never dared to go this far. Sliding his fingers through her strands, pushing them aside so he could keep full contact with her gaze, he rasped, "Maybe this is going to scare you, Kara, but you need to know what's in my heart for you. I fell in love with you the moment I saw you in first grade, even though I didn't know what I felt toward you was called. Later, as I matured, I realized it was puppy love." Grazing her pink cheek, he added in a low, thick tone, "In high school, I continued to love you. But I couldn't have you. Thought I never would."

Her lips compressed and she smoothed her fingers across the fabric of the shirt across his chest. "Because my father said you were beneath me? You figured I deserved someone far better than you? Right?"

His mouth contorted and he looked above her head for a moment before meeting her apologetic gaze. "Yeah, something like that. He stopped short of calling us trailer trash, although after my dad died, we lost our house in bankruptcy and had to find somewhere else to live. He was right about that trailer. But not the trash part."

Reaching up, sliding her fingertips along the line of his jaw, feeling the sandpapery quality of his beard, she whispered, "None of that ever made a difference to me, Cade Patterson. I'm my own person." Her hand stilled against his cheek, drowning in his gold-brown gaze, "I have dreamed my whole life of you being in my life, Cade. Just you. And no matter what man I met after I left at eighteen, none of them could fill your boots."

Blindsided by her admission, he stared down at her, seeing the raw honesty in her eyes. It shook Cade as nothing else had since his father's unexpected death. His hands tightened around her small shoulders and he drowned in her upturned gaze. It was so much to absorb that he was momentarily stunned. He felt her palm gently moving back and forth across his chest, as if in appreciation of him. His throat tightened with overwhelming emotions. "This is a lot to take in," he admitted gruffly.

"I know it is. But it's been inside me for a long, long time, Cade. The only person who can tell me to forget you, forget the dreams I've always had of you, is you." She gave him a tender look. "I used to see you at odd times in the twelve years of school we shared, the way you would look at me sometimes. I knew without a doubt you wanted to know me. I was afraid to call it love because we'd never had any real time together. If my father's spies at school had seen us talk, seen us together in any way, it would have gotten back to him. He swore to hurt any boy who thought he could have me. I didn't want to put you into danger, Cade. And I couldn't even tell you why I wasn't able to come talk to you. I never wanted my father to know that you held my heart. It was my secret."

His whole world anchored and he closed his fingers more surely against her shoulders, still coming to grips with her first admission. Her whispered, choked words flowed into him like sweet, warm honey, awakening his guarded heart, the doors of it flying open, an intense, almost painful sensation flooding him. As Cade searched her gaze, he knew it was true.

"But," he stumbled, his voice low and hoarse, "even now, you're sure you love me, Kara?" How could that be? They'd separated so long ago. So many years stood sterile and empty between them.

Kara gave him a small smile, reaching up, sliding her fingers across his jaw. "You were always my hero, Cade. When you joined the football team and I was a cheerleader, you proved it to me again and again. I knew you were a warrior and you showed it on the field every Friday night during football season. There at least, I could watch you and not get you in trouble with the spies who were always watching me. For all they knew I was just watching the team play as a whole." Her lips twisted with the irony of it. "There were rich boys at school who did their father's bidding and they were all told to pursue me, that they could date me. But if I so much as made eyes at a boy beneath my class, they would tell their father, who would then tell my father and all hell would break loose."

Shaking his head, he rasped, "I didn't know any of this, Kara. I had always thought my wanting you was one way and that you weren't interested in me."

"That's so far from the truth, Cade," she said, leaning up, her palm against his cheek, holding him so that she could kiss him softly.

Cade was torn between Kara's shy kiss

against his mouth and the rage that simmered in him toward Jud Knight and what he'd done to his daughter—and what he'd done to him. What if Jud hadn't put a stranglehold on Kara's heart? What if they could have had a relationship in high school? How would their lives have changed? Would he have gone into the Marine Corps? He'd have had a reason to stay at home and pursue a serious end to his love for Kara. The many dreams he'd had for them, of being in love, getting married, and having a happy, growing family, were too numerous to count throughout those lost years within him.

Slowly, he eased from her wet, sweet mouth, opening his eyes, staring into her half opened ones. There was lust there, no question, but there was also something else: now Cade wasn't afraid to name what he saw. It was love. Kara had loved him from afar all that time, just as he'd loved her. The devastation of how much had been taken from them shattered through Cade. Kara loved him enough to protect him from her vindictive, territorial father.

"This is a lot to absorb," she admitted, her hand coming to rest on his shoulder. "I don't even know what we have, Cade."

Nodding, he felt that furnace of need never more urgent than now. "When I was in grade school, I came home one night and told my dad that I liked you."

"Really?"

"Yeah," Cade admitted, "but I was only six."

"What did your father tell you?"

"He said that sometimes, a special person walks into our life and makes it better. He said when he first met my mother, he felt the same way, although he was eighteen at the time. I told him how funny and happy my heart felt. He said to be a friend to you because friendship was the best basis to find out if what I felt was real and long lasting."

"Your father was so different from mine," she said sadly.

"He had wisdom. I wanted to make you my friend, Kara, but you would never look at me or talk to me. I figured that you didn't like me, so I just stuffed all my feelings into my heart and let you go." He saw pain flash in her eyes, her brows drawing down. "And maybe it was best under the circumstances. Had your father threatened you even then about boys?"

"No, I was six. But when I got into junior high, I guess my hormones changed or I looked at boys differently at that time. The rich boys were already my father's spies and I knew that. But that's when he sat me down and told me he'd hurt any boy who made a move toward me that wasn't from the 'right' family. I got it in spades, then." She shrugged a little. "That's why I redoubled my effort not to look at you, not be seen with you, even in the hallway where the lockers sat."

"You were protecting me?" Cade smoothed his hands against her shoulders, seeing the sadness and hurt in her eyes. Kara had sacrificed so much for him. It shook him, revealing how deep her feelings continued to be for him.

"I did. But I don't regret it, Cade."

"How did you feel when I joined the Marine Corps and left Clayton?" He saw her mouth contort over the question.

"Grief, loss, wishing for a different life, wishing I could get you aside somewhere and tell you how I really felt about you."

He drew Kara fully against him, resting his chin against her hair. "I'm so damned sorry, Kara. I honestly didn't know."

"It's in the past, Cade. We both need to let it go because we can't change it." She pulled back, giving him a firm look. "Like my mom says, you can't cry over spilt milk. When you came back here and joined the sheriff's department, I wanted so badly to approach you, to tell you all of this, but by that time I was afraid."

"Of your father?"

"No, afraid that you didn't love me like I had always loved you. I thought," and she touched her heart, "it was one way. My dream, my need of you. You never approached me and you'd been back from Afghanistan for two years already before you joined the sheriff's department. And so, I finally figured it wasn't the other way around."

He brushed his thumb against her cheek, feeling the softness and that underlying strength that was her. "We silently held the same dream for one another, Kara. I never wavered to this day about how I felt toward you. For me, you were an unreachable dream that was always with me, regardless. I purposely avoided you when I got home. Like you, I thought it was a one-way street. It's nice to know you felt the same way, even though we never had a chance to admit it to one another before this."

"Well," she murmured, stepping out of his arms and gripping his fingers in hers, "all the cards are on the table now, Patterson. I know what I want to do about it. What about you?"

His fingers curved around hers. "I'm all in." He lifted her into his arms. "My bedroom?"

She sighed, looping her arms around his shoulders. "Yes, it's so beautiful in there."

He met her lips, kissing her hungrily. As he lifted away, he growled, "It's *our* bedroom, Kara. You bring your beauty to it as well."

THE NIGHT LIGHT in the hall slanted through the partially opened bedroom door as Cade easily carried her in his arms to his bed. In a way, Kara felt as if this was one of her dreams but this time she was awake to experience it. This was the real thing. Her heart raced with anticipation, fear of not satisfying him, and her undying love for him. Fears of somehow disappointing him with her body, the way she looked, or her skill at lovemaking tunneled through her at the same time. He meant so much to her that she couldn't bear the possibility that he'd be let down by her in some way. Kara had seen the same emotions in his eyes and was grateful that he did not hide himself from her in any way. A fierce love for him swept through her. She was his. Cade had always been hers. Only they hadn't known—but their hearts had.

He placed her gently on the bed so her legs hung over the edge of the mattress. She reached out, her fingers twining with his as he stood next to her. "I'm a mess of emotions, Cade. One second I'm scared and the next, I'm so euphoric I think I could faint from joy. I'm afraid I'll disappoint you in some way. And I love you. The love is so strong in me right now that I can barely think. Is it like that for you?"

She saw instant relief in his expression over her admission, as he recognized she was describing his feelings too.

Releasing her hand, he threaded his fingers through her hair. "Kara, I've never wanted anyone as much as I wanted you. I'm afraid I'll disappoint you, not meet your expectations…things like that." His voice grew thick. "I don't question my love for you because it's never left me."

She gave a partial laugh. "I'm so scared," and she stared up at him, becoming somber. "We've always loved one another. It will be fine, Cade. I know it will, even though I'm as nervous as a high strung horse."

"You have so much courage, Kara. It's going to be fine. We'll do this together at a pace that's right for us."

"I don't think I have very much bravery," she protested. "Just in case you want to know, I'm free of diseases. I'm on an IUD."

"I'm clean, too. Do you want me to wear a condom?"

She shook her head. "No."

He gave her a wry look. "Good thing."

"Why?"

He gave her an amused look. "Because I don't have any," he said, unbuttoning his shirt, pulling it off, revealing the white t-shirt beneath it stretching across his powerful chest.

She sat there watching in appreciation as he undressed without any shyness in front of her. "No condoms because…" she baited, standing and slipping out of her own clothes.

"I've been back here for a year and I was focused on getting settled into my career in law enforcement," he offered, hanging his jeans over the back of a nearby chair. "I'd have had to wait for the drug store to open tomorrow to get them," he said, grinning. Sitting down on the bed next to her, he pulled off his boots, setting them aside. Next came his gray socks. "I wanted this year to adjust to my job, Kara. It wasn't the right time to get into a relationship, if one happened along."

"That's good to know you don't have to go to the drug store," she said, giving him a small smile, taking off her tee. Instead of a bra, she wore a camisole because she was small-breasted. Only if she rode a horse or when she was at work at the Delos Home School, would she wear a bra. Cade's eyes narrowed on the pink silk camisole and she could feel her nipples hardening beneath that flash of heat that came to his eyes. It was a delicious feeling to be adored and desired.

"I don't feel so bad then," she admitted, pulling the camisole off and standing, taking off her bikini panties. "I haven't had sex in over a year, Cade."

"We'll take it slow," he promised, absorbing her from her head down to her toes and then coming back to hold her vulnerable, anxious gaze.

"Good," she whispered, feeling suddenly shaky with need. All Cade had done was give her that hot, hungry look and already there was dampness between her thighs. As he disrobed, she appreciated him all over again. His shoulders, always broad and capable, were powerful looking when he was naked. The dark hair dusted across his well sprung chest, a lean torso, narrow hips and long, powerful thighs. She might have felt overwhelmed by his dark masculinity that had always been hidden from her until now, but instead, a new tenderness swept through her. As she scooted up on the bed, joining him in the center of it, they sat facing one another, their hips meeting. She drowned in his gaze as she slid her hand up his hard thigh, relishing the way his flesh tightened beneath her exploring fingers.

"Tell me what you need," Cade said, slipping his hand from her hip down across her slender leg. "What position do you like best?"

Kara focused on his rough fingers sliding down her flank and said, "It doesn't matter, Cade. Whatever suits us together," she said, staring into his dark, intense eyes, seeing dappled gold in their depths. "We'll be nervous and unsure together."

His hand stilled at her knee, his fingers brushing its inside curve, sending wild, hot sparks upward, making her moan, the pleasure skittering throughout her lower body.

"Kara, you tell me if something I do doesn't feel good to you. Promise?"

She nodded, "I'll speak up. Same goes for me too. I'm not a passive lover."

She saw his lips twitch, that same wicked look coming to his eyes. Sliding his fingers lightly, he continued to ravish that erotic area behind her knee, making her tremble with need of him.

"Fair enough. I've been duly warned."

With a breathy laugh, Kara got to her knees,

placing her hands on his chest. "Lie down," she invited, the teasing amusement in her expression suddenly taking a predatory turn. Cade did as she requested. For so long, she had wanted to touch this man. As he lay back, settling the pillow beneath his head, a lazy, heated look in his eyes, she leaned forward, placing her hands against the thick column of his neck. Hands moving downward, she outlined his shoulders, trailing them back across his collarbones, and then mapping his chest. She was a tactile person, finding great joy by simply touching Cade, hearing a catch in his breath as she swept downward, caressing his erection, and continuing her exploration, memorizing his beautiful male body. He was hers at last. That thrill made her so wet and so ready, it took Kara by surprise. Like most women, she didn't turn on like a light switch. Her sexuality was one of being slowly awakened and cajoled into fiery life.

She massaged his toes and then the arch of his foot, hearing him groan with appreciation from this unexpected pleasure. Kara liked pleasing this man, who had never asked for anything himself. It only made her love Cade more. Time ceased as she once more started at his head, fingers sliding lightly across his scalp, hearing another groan of pleasure. This time she dragged her hardened nipples across his chest, the hard points tangling in his soft, silky hair, and then she stretched forward, her lips seeking his, teasing him unmercifully with her whole body.

The tables were turned when Cade reached outward, wrapping his large hands around her waist, lifting her up and across him, settling her wet, throbbing core on top of his hard erection. The instant her aching center slid across his thick length, she felt a powerful orgasmic explosion within her. Barely aware, she threw her head back, a scream caught in her throat as she was hurled into an incredible galaxy of light and intense pleasure. Cade held her hips, sliding his length against her without entering her, increasing the raw fire coursing throughout her. He kept her from falling, his hands firm, but guiding and pleasing her.

Kara nearly fainted from the throbbing moving throughout her lower body. He hadn't even entered her yet and she was already responding! In her pounding heart, she knew it was because they had secretly loved one another. She knew what sex felt like for sex's sake only. But when emotions were involved and woven with the act, it was unimaginably delicious and satisfying. Cade was her world. He always had been and he always would be.

CHAPTER 7

THERE WAS NOTHING shy or retiring about Kara in his bed and in his arms. She was a tigress taking what she wanted and giving back to him equally. Cade lifted her up again, this time on his erection, sliding deep within her much to their mutual satisfaction. He gave her two more orgasms, one after the other. Her screams sent a spasm of need so deep within Cade that he couldn't hold back as the next orgasm erupted from within her sweet, tight body. Her small hands gripped his shoulders as he thrust hard into her, taking her, feeling that bolt of white hot lightning filling him, filling her. Cade nearly blacked out as he came, hard and strong. He gripped her hips, frozen into timelessness with her as they clung in euphoria, their bodies celebrating this moment that neither thought would ever come in their lifetime.

He caught Kara afterward as she suddenly

collapsed upon him, crying out his name, her body damp as she slumped across him, both of them breathing like the winded animals they'd become. There was nothing like good, primal sex, Cade thought. But with Kara, it amped up to an entirely different level, leaving him panting, his body still throbbing pleasurably in the aftermath. He loved her. When she nuzzled her cheek against his, murmuring his name, licking his neck, nibbling on his earlobe, he surrendered his heart entirely to her. Before this moment, when they'd collided and melted into a oneness that transcended time and space, Cade still felt he was in the best dream of his entire life. He never wanted it to end. Where did dreams meet reality? Could they combine and become real, forever?

He smoothed his hand down her damp spine, her silky hair covering nearly half his face. She smelled of oranges from her favorite soap. The sweetness of her warm flesh and the scent of sex shared between them made his whole body think about loving her all over again. Kara was all softness and curves. It brought every bit of tenderness out of Cade as they lay with one another in the grayness of the room, their silence heavy with celebration and satisfaction.

Later, he eased Kara off him and tucked her beside him on her back so he could prop himself up on one elbow and see the joy alive within her slumberous eyes. It made Cade feel so damned powerful and even more protective toward her than before. He trailed his thumb across her winged brow, watching her expression as she absorbed his touch.

"I love you," he said, his voice low with feelings he could barely contain. "I'll never stop loving you, Kara." He saw tears glimmer in her eyes as she heard his admission.

Kara reached up, smoothing a few strands off his brow. "I'll never stop loving you either, Cade." Her hand stilled on his jaw. "This changes everything. You know that, don't you?"

"Yeah," he grunted, "I do. Your old man is the first on my list to confront. He's going to have to get used to the idea that we're a couple and we're serious with one another whether he likes it or not." He saw her grimace, worry in her eyes. "I'll handle this for us, Kara. I think your mother will be okay with it…"

"Yes, she will be."

"Your father doesn't own you now. He never did."

Nodding, she sighed, leaning over and kissing his chest. "I make it a point to never see him if I can help it. Right now, he and Mom are in Chicago at a cattle breeding conference. They won't get home for about four days if you're thinking of going over to the ranch and telling my father how things are going to be."

"That's good to know. Are you all right with living here with me? I don't want you alone until we can apprehend Fuentes and understand what's going down with his attacks on you."

"I'm fine living here with you, Cade. I feel safer here."

"I'm glad," he murmured, brushing a kiss across her lush lips. "In time, we'll get this all sorted out."

"Sophia's going to have to continue to guard me at Delos then? Follow me to and from work every day?"

"Yes. Until we can find out why you were attacked, Kara, she'll tail you home as well as meet you here every morning to see you make it to Delos without incident. We can't afford to let down our guard."

THE NEXT MORNING, Kara was finishing her third cup of coffee, Cade had just left for work, when the phone rang.

"Hello?"

"Kara, this is Sophia. I've got food poisoning and I'm sicker than a dog. I can't meet you this morning at Cade's home and follow you to Delos. Can you stay there at his home for the day?"

Groaning, Kara said, "Oh, no. I'm sorry you're feeling crappy. Listen, I've got a lot going on this morning at school. We're getting ready for the field trip tomorrow, remember?"

Now it was Sophia's turn to make an unhappy sound. "That's right. I forgot about that. You can't drive there by yourself. I need to tail you, Kara."

"Oh, don't worry it's only twenty miles. Nothing will happen. I'll be fine I'm sure."

"No, don't do that, Kara. Please…"

She smiled. "Listen, you just take it easy, Sophia, and get well. I'll call you when I get to Delos just so you won't worry. Everything will be fine."

Hanging up, Kara hurried through her morning routine and was out the door and into her small, silver KIA Sorrento SUV. It had already begun to rain. At this time of year Texas was dry, so a good storm front coming through, dumping water, was always welcome in the state.

She made sure the house was locked and quickly got into her car, not wanting to be late for work.

Kara was ten miles from the Delos school when her cellphone rang. The highway was empty and the rain heavy, so she was driving more slowly than normal.

"Hello?"

"Kara?"

"Cade! Is something wrong?"

"No, everything's fine at my end. Sophia just called and told me you were taking off by yourself to go to Delos. I'm five minutes behind you. I'll escort you the rest of the way to your school."

"Oh I'm sorry, Cade. I felt I'd be safe enough and could drive without an escort just this once."

"Sweetheart, until we resolve what's going on with Fuentes we can't take a chance."

Kara gasped, suddenly aware that a chromed black pickup truck with a lot of chrome trim on it was racing up behind her. Its bumper loomed in her rear window. She dropped the phone, grabbing the steering wheel with both hands. He was going to hit her!

The pickup slammed into her left rear fender and the jolt jerked Kara. The noise was like a thunderclap around her. The seat belt bit into her shoulder. The airbags deployed. In seconds, she was spinning around and around as the car skidded off the wet highway. It leapt over the berm, slamming her hard down into her seat. She saw a flash of the black truck racing by her, headed toward Clayton.

Another cry tore out of her as her SUV canted and slid down the wet, slippery embankment, coming to rest against a rancher's barbed wire fence below.

Everything went suddenly quiet.

Breathing harshly, Kara was dazed by the suddenness of the attack. Thank God she was wearing her seat belt. She pushed the air bag away from her face, trying to see where she was at.

"Kara!"

She jerked to the left, seeing Cade outside

her car window, his face grim, eyes wide with concern. Quickly, she opened the door after struggling to get the air bag out of the way.

"Cade—"

He crouched down between the car door and the frame, his hand on her shoulder. "Are you all right? Are you injured?"

"N-no, just shook up. Someone hit me from behind on purpose."

"Yeah," he growled. "I saw it. I've just called it in. I need you to come with me, Kara. Can you walk?" He quickly took the seat belt off her, giving her his hand. She nodded and jerkily extricated herself out of the car, in shock.

"W-what are you going to do?" she asked, giving her car a look. The trunk was smashed in, the rear window shattered. She could have died.

Cade was wearing his dark brown nylon jacket to keep dry and he tucked her beneath his arm, leading her quickly up the bank to where his cruiser was parked. "We're going after that truck. Hurry! Climb in!"

In moments, she was in the passenger side of the cruiser. The light bar on top of the vehicle flashed its red and blue lights. He helped her put on the seatbelt then got in, slamming the car into gear, wheels spinning as he aimed it back onto the shining black asphalt highway.

She hung on, her heart pounding. "W-who was that? Who hit me?"

"I don't know," he growled, slowly accelerating the cruiser on the slick highway. What he didn't want to do was start hydroplaning and then lose control of the vehicle. "I've got four cruisers coming up fast on me from the sheriff's department. We're going to try and locate the black truck and finish this off, one way or another. I've alerted U.S. Border Patrol at the other end of the highway and they're ready to stop them if they get that far. They're not getting across the border."

A CHILL BOLTED through Kara as she hung on, her hair damp around her face. Pushing strands away from her cheek with trembling fingers she said, "I'm sorry, Cade. I should have listened to Sophia and stayed home. I honestly thought it would be safe to drive twenty miles to my school. I really did."

"It's all right. Sophia called me right away after you two hung up with one another. I happened to be at the station, getting ready for my shift. No harm, no foul." He gave her a quick look of reassurance.

"I just didn't think I'd get attacked again," she whispered lamely, giving him a woeful look.

"We've got to find out what the hell is going on," he told her grimly, his gaze riveted to the wet, rainy highway.

Kara saw the posts go from wood to white

metal pipe fence, indicating they were now flying down the road, paralleling her father's huge, sprawling ranch. "There's the truck that hit me!" she cried out, pointing out the windshield.

"Yeah, I see it," Cade said, grim satisfaction in his tone.

"Look!" she yelped in disbelief. "They're turning into the main entrance of my father's ranch! What's going on here, Cade?"

Cade shrugged, speaking into his radio, giving the deputies who were racing to catch up with him the update. Signing off the radio, he began slowing down, braking to make the turn over the wide cattle guard. "I don't know what's going on, Kara. Maybe they think they can run onto anyone's ranch and try to escape us." His lips thinned. "It's not going to work." He swung the cruiser through the entrance, watching the truck fishtail ahead of them on the slippery asphalt. Every deputy familiarized him or herself with the ranches in Kenedy County. He recalled the layout on the Knight ranch, knowing there was an asphalt road to the main house and about half a mile down, the barn area. The rain had stopped and he saw the white two-story home up ahead and three red barns sitting half a mile behind it.

On either side of the road were fenced pipe rail pastures. In one, there was a small herd of white Santa Gertrudis cows with young calves.

"Where are they going?" Kara demanded, leaning forward, eyes narrowing as she watched the pickup continue at high speed toward her parents' home.

"I have no idea," Cade said, glancing in her direction. "They may be trying to lose me."

"Well," Kara muttered, "that asphalt road turns into a dirt road at the three barns area. If they think they're going to lose you on that muddy dirt road, it gets really slippery after a rain. They can't speed or they'll crash, Cade."

"My thoughts exactly. Listen, you need to stay with the cruiser if they stop and bail. All right?"

"Oh, I'm not getting out," she promised, giving him a worried look. She frowned. "They're turning into the barn area. What gives?"

Cade didn't know, tightening his hands on the wheel, slowing down as they quickly approached the ranch home. He saw several wranglers in one pasture on horseback, herding a group of cattle toward another area in the distance. There were two wranglers in the ranch yard, doing clean up duties. Everything looked normal and quiet, but it wasn't.

His mind churned with possibilities. Once more, Cade got on the radio, advising the deputies where the suspect was headed at the Circle K. They would arrive within minutes.

"They've stopping at barn three!" Kara gasped, giving Cade a wide-eyed look of confusion.

"Isn't that the barn you said was off limits to

you by your father?"

"Yes, yes it was. I don't know what's inside it. I never went in to find out."

Cade saw the truck screech to a halt. Two men with rifles as well as pistols on their hips, leaped out, running hard for the closest door to the barn. "Stay in the cruiser, Kara, no matter what happens. Don't leave it. If they start shooting, get down on the floorboards and keep your head down."

"I-I won't leave this car. Why are they running inside the barn? I don't understand this. They act like they *know* our ranch and that barn. This doesn't make sense, Cade."

Hearing the confusion in her strained voice, he said, "We're going to find out." He braked the cruiser no more than ten feet away from the pickup. Both men had already disappeared inside the barn.

It was three-stories tall. What the hell was in there? Cade knew he was in danger by going in after them alone and he needed back up, but he wasn't willing to wait. Wearing a Kevlar vest beneath his khaki shirt, he quickly parked the cruiser.

"When Burt Larson and the rest of the deputies arrive, they'll follow me in and give me backup. You stay put. Tell them what you know."

Giving a nod, she gripped his arm. "Be careful, Cade! Please! God, don't get hurt!"

"I'll be okay," he promised, unsnapping the

harness, pushing open the door, and un-
holstering his pistol. "Lock the car doors behind
me." He saw how frightened Kara was. Sweeping
the area, he saw no other wranglers nearby. He
clicked on the radio attached to his shoulder
epaulet and alerted the deputies on their way that
he was entering barn three to apprehend the two
fleeing suspects. He gave clear details about
which barn it was and the weapons the men were
carrying. The air was humid and warm, and Cade
was already starting to sweat as he swept the
immediate area for other intruders. Then, he
raced toward the small, opened door to barn
three. He could hear the lowing of some cattle, a
bark of a dog within the white picket fence of the
main ranch house. Everything seemed so
peaceful.

He worried about the two men as he raced
into the entrance of barn three. Who on earth
were they? Did they work here? His mind spun
with questions as he pressed himself to the door
jamb, swiftly looking from side to side as he
entered, pistol drawn.

The barn was huge and airy, light pouring in
from various windows above from the second
and third story of the building. It was grayish
light though, which made it hard to see things
clearly. His heart was racing as he kept his hands
around his pistol and silently slipped inside.
Hunkering down behind bales of straw stacked
near the door, he heard the rough panting of the

men echoing throughout the structure. Their boots struck a floor above him, the thunking sounds reverberating throughout it. His nostrils flared as he caught another scent. Damned if it wasn't the odor of marijuana! Swiveling his head, Cade saw another group of what appeared to be bales of alfalfa. They were stacked in dark green plastic, to the rear of the first floor, which was where the smell was originating.

However, Cade didn't have time to check it out. Leaping to his feet, he rapidly covered the distance to a barn ladder attached to the side of the southern wall. It was the only way up to the second and third stories of this place. Where the hell were they going? What did they know that he didn't? Making sure he moved silently, he quickly ascended the ladder, pushing his pistol into his holster first. Barely easing his head to eye level with the second floor, he saw the two men hurriedly scrambling up the ladder to the third floor.

Grimacing, he took advantage of the situation, throwing himself up on the floor and running quietly to the north side of the barn where that ladder was situated. Neither suspect was looking back to see if someone was following them. That either spoke of their overblown confidence or their stupidity, he couldn't decide which. It didn't matter anyway. It played into his hands.

Below, Cade heard other men's voices. The

deputies had arrived. The men disappeared, clunking across the wooden floor, weaving in and around huge lots of bales that were wrapped in dark green plastic. The smell of marijuana was intense up here. Leaping off the ladder, slipping off to one side, Cade gave Burt his position. He didn't want them shooting at him. Burt informed him that he'd already placed a deputy at the other two entrance/exit points on the first floor of the barn because Kara had told him about them. The rest of the law enforcement officers were coming inside with Burt to join him.

Satisfied, Cade waited for his team to arrive. Only one man at a time could ascend those ladders. Where the hell were they going? What was up on the third floor? Wiping the sweat off his brow with the back of his arm, he waited impatiently, hearing the echo of deputies' heavy boots coming up the ladder to the second floor. The cavalry had finally arrived.

KARA SAT TENSELY in the cruiser, her hand pressed against her throat, her gaze riveted on the door of barn three. One grim-looking deputy, armed with an assault weapon, stood guard next to it, keeping watch. She'd seen two other deputies race around the barn with the same weapon, wearing Kevlar vests, heading for the other barn exit points. Her heart wouldn't stop pounding and all she could think of was Cade and the other deputies being in danger. Cade had just gotten together with her for the first time in their lives. Would they have another day together? Terror ate at her as she twisted and moved restlessly in the passenger seat.

Two of her father's wranglers had come over after all the sheriff's cruisers had parked near the barn area. She told them to stay with her and not go near the barn. In as few words as possible through the opened window, she explained what had happened. The two cowboys looked worried and confused by the unexpected intrusion, but remained steadfastly by the cruiser with her, more in a protective stance, which Kara appreciated. They weren't armed, but she was grateful they remained nearby.

Her mind whirled with so many questions. Neither cowboy had recognized the black truck or its occupants as it had raced by where they had been working in the front yard of the main ranch house. One part of her was glad her parents were in Chicago for the conference and not here to see this happen. She knew her father's pompous stance in regards to law-enforcement and he would have been a pain in the ass to the deputies here on a manhunt. Word spread fast on a ranch this size and Kara knew that all the wranglers carried a radio. She didn't know where the foreman was but she was sure he was getting word out to all the employees about what was going down.

Suddenly, shots rang out in the barn.

Kara jumped. A squeal of surprise tore from her.

Both wranglers tensed as well, crouching near the cruiser, their gazes locked on the barn in front of them. The deputy standing guard tensed, rifle aimed at the door.

Oh God! Never had Kara prayed as hard as she did right now. *Don't let Cade get hurt. Please God, protect him! I love him so much! Let us have a life together!* The litany spun around and around inside her head as she stared at the barn.

More shots rang out.

Kara squelched her cry. It sounded like a war was going on inside the barn!

She wanted to get out and run in there, but she knew better. The wranglers had moved to either side of the cruiser, like guardians protecting her, telling her to get down on the floorboards and cover her head, which she instantly did. They remained at each main door of the cruiser, hunkering down as bullets flew around the area.

Then, there was complete silence. Kara cautiously lifted her head, her eyes huge. Both the wranglers slowly straightened, intently watching the now quiet barn. Cautiously, Kara dragged herself off the floorboards, eyes trained on the barn. Was someone hurt? What was going on? She swallowed hard, her throat dry, her heart beating so hard she could barely hear because of it.

It was a long ten minutes after the last gun-fire had erupted before she saw Cade emerge from the barn with an angry-looking Fuentes in handcuffs. Cade had his game face on and she anxiously scanned it as he pushed the thug toward the other four cruisers behind his own, his gun drawn.

A moment later, a second man in handcuffs was pushed out of the entrance by Burt. The rest of the deputies joined them and they marched the men toward two different cruisers, making them get into the rear of each one.

Kara pushed the door open, seeing Cade coming her way as he holstered his weapon after handing Fuentes off to a deputy at one of the cruisers. He was breathing hard, sweat gleaming on his face. The moment their eyes met and locked, she called his name, wanting to run to him, but forcing herself to walk instead. He met her and although they couldn't show any affection for one another under the circumstances, his game face dissolved.

"I'm okay," he rasped, keeping his voice low as they stood a few feet apart. "I love you, Kara. Everything's going to be all right."

"I was so scared," she said, choking back the rest. His slacks were dusty, some straw on them here and there. The armpits of his khaki shirt were stained dark with sweat. His hair was mussed, but he looked fine. He was alive!

Cade gestured to the cruiser. "The dispatcher has called a wrecker to come and pick up your car alongside the highway. They'll take it to the garage in Clayton. You and I need to go back to HQ. I have to fill out a report on what happened and you have to give a statement. Are you up to it?" He gave her a long, intent look.

"Yes, that's fine. Has someone from your side called my parents yet? I have my father's cellphone number if you need it. One of the wrangler's who protected me at your cruiser had a call from the foreman. He's already called my father in Chicago to report what's going on here."

Cade pulled out his cellphone. "Give it to me. I'll have the dispatcher get hold of them and let them know what happened. He needs to hear it from us, not from his foreman."

"What will you do after you write up the report on their truck striking my car?"

"We'll take the two perps back to headquarters. We've already got two FBI agents from Houston there because of another case, and they'll interrogate them. I'm the officer on record for this arrest and I don't know how long I'll be there. Sometimes, these interrogations can go on for hours. Long hours. Unless they both lawyer up."

"Do you think they're American citizens?"

"Hell no," he snorted. "We have U.S. Immigration and Customs Enforcement, coming to pay them a visit as well. My guess is that they're here illegally. Never mind that they tried to kill you, there's going to be a boat load of felonies thrown at them." He walked to the cruiser and opened the door for her. Already, the two men were being driven back to Sarita for interrogation. As he climbed into the cruiser, his cellphone rang and he answered it.

Kara heard him talking to the dispatcher. It was a short conversation. Afterward, he turned to Kara. "Dispatch just contacted your father. Your parents are flying back home on the first available flight. They'll let us know when they land in Houston."

Nodding, she said, "Okay. My father will have his helicopter pilot meet them in Houston and fly them back here to the ranch."

"Are you going to meet them?"

"No. I hardly ever come back to this ranch, Cade. This shootout doesn't change how I feel. I'm just glad neither of them were here to witness it."

He reached out, squeezing her hands that were gripped tightly in her lap. "Well, depending upon how the interrogation goes and what we find out, your father and mother may get pulled into this whether they want to or not."

Her eyes widened. "Why? They were gone. How could they be involved?"

He took a deep breath and said quietly, "When I went into barn three, I found thousands of pounds of marijuana in huge bales, covered in plastic awaiting shipment. Burt found at least five hundred pounds of cocaine in another place on the third floor. It was wrapped in one kilo black plastic bags and stored in a corner. There are a lot of drugs being kept in that barn, Kara. I'm sorry," he said, searching her stricken looking face.

"Oh, no…"

"Do you think that's why your father made barn three off limits to you?"

"I-I don't know. Oh, this is shocking!"

"What about your mother? Do you think she knew about your father's drug activities?"

Tears came to her eyes and Kara forced them back. "No. My mother would never be involved in something like this!" She rubbed her face, trying to control herself. "My father, I'd believe it, Cade. I really would. I told you his history. Maybe he made Mom and I think that he'd quit dealing drugs at eighteen but maybe he didn't," she said, holding his grim looking gaze. And then, a realization struck her. "Oh no! Will the FBI think I'm involved in this too, Cade?"

He gave her an apologetic look. "They're going to look at everything, Kara. But don't worry. I know you're not involved. But it does mean they will talk with you too. Just tell the truth and don't hold anything back from them. It will help them understand the dynamics between you and your family." His hand tightened over hers. "It will be all right. I'm here. I'll be with you every step of the way on this."

Kara managed a wobbly smile and as Cade released her hand, she forced herself to control her rampant feelings. She wondered if her father knew what had happened. How much had the dispatcher told Cade? Her stomach was still clenched from the shoot-out in the barn. She recognized Fuentes, who had crashed into her SUV. Feeling torn, but she knew Cade had duties to attend to and she would be questioned by the FBI at the sheriff's headquarters.

What had possessed those two men to hole up in barn three in the first place? She couldn't shake the grim look in Cade's eyes either. It was as if he were holding back a lot of emotions, a lot of information. But she couldn't read his mind, as much as she wanted to. Tonight when he finally got home, they would talk. Then she'd find out a lot more about Fuentes and why he was still after her. This was an unraveling nightmare to Kara and she was dizzied by the information Cade had given her. Was her father really into dealing drugs?

Her left arm near her elbow was badly bruised from the auto accident and she cupped it, the heat feeling good on it. That was the only injury she'd sustained from her car being hit and spinning out of control. It was enough. How badly she ached to be at home with Cade. Alone. Only with him.

CHAPTER 8

I T WAS SIX p.m. and Cade was trying to gird himself emotionally with the coming information he had to give to Kara. The FBI had talked to her and released her by late morning, but they had asked her to remain in Cade's office in case they wanted to talk with her again later. Her parents had arrived at the sheriff's office. The FBI would not allow them to meet one another, keeping them separated. Kara was understandably upset but understood. She found out that the FBI, ICE, the DEA, U.S. Border Patrol, and now ATF, were involved. The search by the FBI in barn three revealed a cache of long rifles, among them, AK-47s.

The Kenedy County Sheriff's Department building wasn't that large to begin with but now, it was cramped with law enforcement staff, agents, officers, and suspects. Wiping his mouth, he opened his office where Kara was patiently waiting for him. She looked stressed, her eyes dark. She'd been through a hell of a lot today.

"Can I see Mom now?" she asked hopefully, sitting up in the chair behind his desk.

With a shake of his head, he quietly shut the door. "No, not yet. How are you holding up? Would you like another bottle of water?"

"No, I'm okay. You look so tired, Cade."

He was tired to his soul because of what he was going to have to share with her.

"I need to go over some things with you, Kara." He came around the desk and pulled up a second chair, taking her hands in his as he faced her. "The good news is that you're not a suspect in this case." He saw instant relief in her eyes. "From everything I'm hearing, and this isn't approved yet but will be shortly, your mother is not a suspect either."

More relief came to her face. His hands tightened around her damp fingers.

"Fuentes, when the FBI agent started to interrogate him, made a mistake that the agent caught." Releasing her hand, he pulled up the sleeve, exposing his wrist. "Fuentes demanded to make a call to a lawyer first thing. We have to legally honor that request. The agent nodded and then saw him look at the inside of his left wrist. The man has tattoos from each of his wrists to his shoulders and his neck," Cade said. "The agent saw the number. He got up and gave Fuentes the phone to make the call. Afterward, the agent ran the number." His voice lowered.

"Kara, it was your father's private cellphone number."

Her brows flew up and she gasped. Pulling her other hand from his, she said, "My father isn't a lawyer. Why would Fuentes call him?"

"That's what the FBI agent wanted to know. Fuentes would say nothing except that his attorney would be here shortly." Wincing inwardly, Cade saw the terrible reality land on Kara.

"Then Fuentes is someone who works for my father? He never got out of the drug business did he, Cade?"

"Doesn't look like it." He reached for her hand, holding her grief-stricken gaze. "I'm sorry, Kara. You didn't deserve this. Neither did your mother. She didn't have a clue about your father's covert activities, either."

"Then," she wobbled, "did my father send Fuentes to attack me? To what end? I don't understand."

"Remember when I was in the hospital with you and your father came to visit you?"

"Yes."

"He told you that you'd be safer on the ranch, that you should come back and live there with them. He wanted to teach you to be the foreman of it someday. Do you remember that conversation?" Because Cade had never forgotten the bastard's demeanor toward his only daughter. Even now, it made him angry. Kara's gaze went from grief stricken to utterly shocked.

"Oh...no, Cade. No, he wouldn't do that to me! He couldn't have sent Fuentes after me hoping that it would scare me back to the ranch, back to him." And then she placed her hand against her lips, staring at him with anguish as the truth sunk in.

"That's what we all think, although your father isn't saying a word. Fuentes however, is going to turn evidence on your father over to the FBI and tell them everything he knows. He's going for a plea deal. He said your father hired him to scare you," Cade told her quietly, seeing tears form in her eyes. How badly he wanted to protect her but this time, he couldn't. It made Cade feel helpless in a way he never wanted to feel.

Kara was the innocent in all of this. And never had she looked as devastated as she did right now.

"I-I don't want to believe it, Cade. He never lifted a hand to me while I was growing up."

"He didn't have to, sweetheart. He abused you in other ways to keep you under his control." She closed her eyes, the corners of her mouth pulling inward for a moment. "I wish...I wish I could make this go away, Kara, but this is a nightmare for you and your mom."

Opening her eyes, she stared at him. "My poor mother. What must she be going through?

To be deceived like that, Cade. And lied to? Our whole life was a complete sham."

"We're just at the tip of this investigation. Your father has lawyered up. It's going to be on law enforcement's shoulders to prove he's a major drug running player. Remember those illegal immigrants you saw that night when you were ten-years-old? And that little boy who got his arm broken for running away because he was scared?"

"Yes?"

"The FBI thinks your father was a regional hub for illegal immigrants coming across the border, a coyote of sorts. He probably got paid by the head."

Kara eased to her feet and walked slowly around the office, her arms around her waist, holding herself.

Cade stood and took her into his arms, wanting to give her something…anything, to ease her pain. To his great relief, she sighed, slid her arms around his waist and snuggled against his chest. He could feel her weariness and worse, her shame over her father's secret, double life.

"He blindsided us," she mumbled against his shirt. "Mom and I didn't have a clue."

"Yeah, he blindsided the people he supposedly loved," Cade agreed hoarsely, kissing her temple, sliding his hand through her hair, needing to give her some kind of comfort. Knowing that in the coming months, maybe even years, her family's name was going to be dragged through the mud in the national news. It was just another heavy burden Kara had to carry. But she wouldn't have to do it alone. He would be at her side, carrying it with her every step of the way.

THE COOL NOVEMBER evening made Kara put on a sweater as she sat outside on the porch swing at Cade's home. The sun was setting, the sky torn with clouds heralding the late-season hurricane that had entered the Gulf a day ago. Rain and wind were in the forecast. She sat there using the toe of her shoe to push the large wooden swing slowly back and forth. The last three months of her life had been the worst and the best she'd ever experienced.

Cade nudged the door open with the toe of his cowboy boot, balancing two cups of hot chocolate with whipped cream in his hands.

Kara smiled, taking one cup, thanking him. He came and sat next to her, placing his arm around her shoulders, drawing her against him. "You're my dessert," she murmured, lifting her chin, meeting and holding the warmth in his light brown gaze. "Thank you."

"Every day with you is a gift to me, Kara" he said. Looking down at the engagement ring on her left hand, he added, "I don't know how I lived without you in my life. I really don't."

Her body glowed with the memory of them making love an hour earlier. She took a sip of the chocolate, setting it on a nearby table. Then, she nestled against him. "Me either," she murmured, pressing a kiss into the black polo shirt he wore. "I'm so happy with you, Cade," she said, melting beneath the burning look of love that he gave her. "Despite everything, I've never been happier."

"Good, because it's gotten pretty bad of late," he mumbled, taking a sip of the hot chocolate, licking his lips free of the whipped cream.

She smiled, lifting her finger, removing a bit from his upper lip. "Mmmm…you make everything we do sensual and erotic, you know that?" She opened her lips, licking the cream off her finger, watching his eyes narrow on her, feeling his alpha male response.

"Because we have how many years of yearning stored up for one another? Now, for the first time in our lives, we're really getting to share how we felt about one another all those years," Cade teased, giving her a swift, hot kiss on the mouth. He felt her smile beneath his mouth as he slowly parted from her lips, seeing the joy dancing in her eyes.

"Maybe," she agreed equitably, content to take another sip of her hot chocolate.

"How's your mom doing adjusting to being boss of the ranch?"

"Surprisingly well. At first, after Father was indicted, I didn't know if she was going to make it. But she turned a corner and she's doing fine now. She asked us to join her for Thanksgiving. Are you up for that? She invited your mom too."

"How do you feel about it? I know when you go to the ranch the bad memories come back."

Shrugging, she said, "Mom had an important 'aha' moment for me the other day on the phone, Cade. She said that she'd fallen out of love with my father after I was born. He wanted only her, not her child. She stayed in that loveless marriage because of me and I found that sad, but I didn't say that to her. It was confounding her that he wanted me back on the ranch when he'd never wanted me at all. When she found out from the FBI that he'd hired Fuentes to 'scare' me into coming back to the ranch, she filed for a divorce. Now, he's a stranger to her—someone she no longer knows. He's in jail in Houston awaiting trial, with no bond set. The more we both found out about his deep drug roots, the easier it was for me to completely release myself from him. Mom said I was not guilty in any of this. That I took from the best of his genes, not the worst. She saw how important Delos was to me, and how happy I was. She wanted me to know that she fully supported all my choices in life."

"Good to hear," Cade murmured. "That took a lot of courage on her part, too."

"Yes, it did. But I can't imagine being in a

loveless marriage with a man who was so dark, who lied to her constantly, and hid from her his real business, which was drugs, weapons, and trafficking."

Squeezing her shoulders gently, he said gruffly, "Your mom did the best she could, and on the plus side, the ranch is starting to thrive. She's hired new wranglers to replace the ones in cahoots with your father's drug business. I think she's happy and she's fully capable of running that ranch."

"I took the liberty of calling your mom," she said, holding his gaze. "She's more than willing to bury the hatchet between the two families. She's glad to be starting over with all of us."

"That's good," Cade said, finishing off the hot chocolate and placing the mug on a nearby table. "I'd like to go to the ranch for Turkey Day," he said, smiling at her. "Are you going to make pumpkin pies? The one you made a month ago was really good."

Laughing, she nodded. "For you? Anything."

CADE KNEW THE depth of courage and strength that Kara possessed as never before. When the news story hit about Jud Knight being the second-in-command within the Gomez drug cartel on the U.S. side of the multi-country operation, he watched the devastation, the shock, and hurt move through Kara daily. But like her Texan mother, and like all Texas born women he knew, they had titanium spines. Within a week, the famous Knight ranch became an embarrassment to the state. People who had known Knight were surprised and didn't want to believe it. But as more and more evidence was produced, the world accepted the rich man's illegal schemes. Luckily, Kara and her mother were not muddied in the screaming headlines. They were just the collateral damage and of little interest to the news hounds.

And Cade was glad because Kara was fragile after that for a couple of months, but her mother was a stanchion of strength for her, and so was he. Between the two of them Kara was rediscovering her own core strength and balance. She had children's lives to guide, a day care center that helped so many working class parents. Each day when she returned to Cade's home, he could see how helping these children helped her recover too. The love they effortlessly bestowed upon Kara was doing its healing work. Cade was there for her as she cried when she had nightmares, or when she felt abandoned by her larger-than-life, controlling father. The blindsiding had deeply wounded both women, but like the Texans they were, they fought back and found a deeper strength to continue to move forward.

Cade and Kara were going to marry on February 14th, Valentine's Day. It was all heart's day, in Cade's way of thinking and seeing the world. Both mothers had become good friends over the course of the last few months, planning Kara's wedding with him. And that made his heart sing. As he swung with her, watching her sip the rich hot chocolate, watching that diamond engagement ring glint in the evening dusk coming upon them, he'd never felt happier or more fulfilled.

Cade found their life paths crisscrossing so many times and yet, because of Kara's father, they'd split apart from one another. Sometimes, he woke up at night after making love with her, amazed at how they had found one another once again, despite the man's machinations. Their hearts yearned to be together, regardless of time, place, or space. He loved Kara with his life and always would. The dreams they dreamed together now were incredible and were filled with such hope and love. He pressed a kiss to her hair, never happier, never more fulfilled.

THE END

Don't miss Lindsay McKenna's next DELOS
series novella,

**Secret Dream, 1B, novella epilogue to
Nowhere to Hide**

Available from Lindsay McKenna and Blue
Turtle Publishing and wherever you buy eBooks!

Turn the page for a sneak peek of *Secret Dream!*

Excerpt from

Secret Dream

"CAV! THERE'S MY mom and dad!" She practically ran toward them, dragging him along with her. Though she was a tiny little thing, Cav had learned early on she wasn't weak.

Cav saw a tall, darkly tanned man in a straw cowboy hat, a chambray shirt, jeans, and work boots standing next to a woman. She had blond hair and was wearing a short-sleeved white blouse, jeans, and flat, sensible leather shoes. He saw their faces light up when they spotted Lia.

"Hey," he called to Lia, "go to them. I'll follow." He released her hand but she turned, giving him a pouty look.

"I'm not leaving you behind!" Lia grabbed at his hand once more, turning and urging him to hurry along. Cav broke out into a self-conscious grin as he saw her parents watching their exchange. Is this what a family did when a stranger was brought along, dragged hurriedly to them? Cav felt out of place, uncomfortable, as he saw Lia's mother scowl, her green eyes narrowing judgmentally upon him. He hoped what he was wearing didn't make her think he wasn't worthy of Lia. Because the way she was sizing him up, Cav felt the full impact of her all-terrain radar, which was focused solely on him. He'd worn bone-colored chinos, a bright red polo shirt, and a black baseball cap. He'd purposely kept his dark glasses hanging out of his shirt pocket. As a SEAL, he would always wear them, but Lia complained constantly that she loved to look into his hazel eyes, not see her reflection in his shades. Cav had to remind himself that he wasn't in PSD—personal security detail—mode, that he was with the woman he loved. Lia was practically jumping up and down now, hurrying to reach her parents, who were smiling widely. That was a relief. Susan Cassidy could smile. That laserlike look she'd given him was gone now. *Phew.*

"Mom! Dad!" Lia cried out. She dragged Cav over to them. "This is Cav Jordan. Cav? My dad, Steve Cassidy. My mom, Susan."

She released Cav's right hand. He awkwardly extended it toward Susan. "Mrs. Cassidy, it's nice to meet you." He felt her stare icily at him, as if he were some alien who had just come from outer space. Reluctantly, she proffered her hand, barely shaking his.

"Nice to meet you, Mr. Jordan."

He felt that limp handshake of hers and tried to make the best of it, but the vibe from her wasn't good. *Great.*

"Call him Cav, Mom," Lia pleaded, launching

herself at her mother, throwing her arms around her.

Cav stood back, watching mother and daughter embrace one another. All of that ice melted instantly as Susan grabbed her shorter daughter and held her strongly in her arms. The love was clearly written in her face. Cav swallowed hard. For a moment, he pictured his mother, who, when he was a young child, had hauled him into her arms and held him just as tightly as Susan was holding her daughter.

The Books of Delos

Title: ***Last Chance*** (Prologue)
Publish Date: July 15, 2015
Learn more at:
delos.lindsaymckenna.com/last-chance

Title: ***Nowhere to Hide***
Publish Date: October 13, 2015
Learn more at:
delos.lindsaymckenna.com/nowhere-to-hide

Title: ***Tangled Pursuit***
Publish Date: November 11, 2015
Learn more at:
delos.lindsaymckenna.com/tangled-pursuit

Title: ***Forged in Fire***
Publish Date: December 3, 2015
Learn more at:
delos.lindsaymckenna.com/forged-in-fire

Title: ***Broken Dreams***
Publish Date: January 2, 2016
Learn more at:
delos.lindsaymckenna.com/broken-dreams

Everything Delos!

Newsletter

Please sign up for my free quarterly newsletter on the front page of my official Lindsay McKenna website at lindsaymckenna.com. The newsletter will have exclusive information about my books, publishing schedule, giveaways, exclusive cover peeks, and more.

Delos Series Website

Be sure to drop by the website dedicated to the Delos series at delos.lindsaymckenna.com. There will be new articles on characters, publishing schedule and information about each book written by Lindsay.

Quote Books

I love how the Internet has evolved. I had great fun create "quote books with text" which reminded me of an old fashioned comic book…lots of great color photos and a little text, which forms a "book" that tells you, the reader, a story. Let me know if you like these quote books because I think it's a great way to add extra enjoyment with this series! Just go to my Delos Series website delos.lindsaymckenna. com, which features the books in the series.

The individual downloadable quote books are located on the corresponding book pages. Please share with your reader friends!

Follow the history of Delos:

The video quote book will lead you through the

history of how and why Delos was formed. You can also download the quote book as a PDF.

The Culver Family History
The history of the Culver Family, featuring Robert and Dilara Culver, and their children, Tal, Matt and Alexa will be available as a downloadable video or PDF quote book.

Nowhere to Hide, **Book 1, Delos Series, October 13, 2015**
This quote book will lead you through Lia Cassidy's challenges in Costa Rica and hunky Cav Jordan, ex-SEAL. Download the book and enjoy more of the story.

Tangled Pursuit, **Book 2, Delos Series, November 11, 2015**
This quote book will introduce you to Tal Culver and her Texas badass SEAL warrior who doesn't take "no" for an answer.

Forged in Fire, **Book 3, Delos Series, December 3, 2015**
This quote book will introduce you to Army Sergeant Matt Culver, Delta Force operator and Dr. Dara McKinley.

Broken Dreams, **Book 4, Delos Series, January 2, 2016**
This quote book will introduce you to Captain Alexa Culver and Marine Sergeant Gage Hunter, sniper, USMC.

Made in the USA
Middletown, DE
17 January 2017